SCHOOL of SECRETS

ALLY'S
MAD MYSTERY

JESSICA BRODY

DISNEP PRESS

Los Angeles • New York

Printed in the United States of America
First Hardcover Edition, February 2017
First Paperback Edition, February 2017
1 3 5 7 9 10 8 6 4 2
FAC-020093-17013

Library of Congress Control Number: 2016939521
Hardcover ISBN 978-1-4847-7866-1
Paperback ISBN 978-1-4847-9931-4

For more Disney Press fun, visit www.disneybooks.com
Visit DisneyDescendants.com

SUSTAINABLE FORESTRY INITIATIVE   Certified Sourcing
www.sfiprogram.org
SFI-00993

THIS LABEL APPLIES TO TEXT STOCK

MORE NEW BOOKS COMING SOON IN
THE SCHOOL OF SECRETS SERIES . . .

NEXT:
LONNIE'S
WARRIOR SWORD

A Very Curious Souvenir

The object looked old. Older than anything the girl had ever seen before. Nothing rusted in Auradon. Nothing squeaked or cracked or weathered with age. Everything in the magical kingdom was always shiny and bright and sparkling.

But not this.

This was tarnished and worn. The gold metal surface seemed to have lost its sheen many years before.

As the young girl watched her mother carefully remove the object from her desk, drawing it out by its long golden chain, her eyes grew wide with wonder.

"What is it, Mummy?" she asked.

It was obvious her mother hadn't realized the girl was watching her from the doorway, because she startled slightly at the sound of her daughter's voice and then turned to give her a warm smile.

"This is a souvenir from a very curious time in my life. I'm trying to find a safe place to keep it. Would you like to see it?"

The girl's face brightened with unbridled excitement. She nodded and ran eagerly toward her mother, her arms swinging with delight, but her mother extended a hand to stop her, putting a safe distance between the girl and the mysterious object.

"Slow down, my darling," she warned the girl. "You are always in much too much of a hurry. You must be gentle with this. It's very old and quite fragile."

The girl leaned over her mother's arm to get a better look at the round gold object dangling from the chain.

"You see," her mother explained, daintily cradling the trinket in her palm and turning it over so the girl could see the front, "it's a pocket watch."

The girl tilted her head and studied the watch, gazing at the faded black numbers—one through twelve—arranged in a circle beneath a thin sheet of glass. She listened to the faint *tick, tick, tick* it made against her mother's palm.

"It has a peculiar-sounding heartbeat," the girl noted, and her mother let out a jubilant laugh.

"That's not its heart, my dear. That's the second hand, keeping time. Making sure you're never late. If that ticking were to ever stop, it would mean the watch was broken."

The girl looked confused for a moment. "Isn't that the same as a heartbeat?"

Her mother chuckled. "I suppose you're right." She reached out and brushed a strand of her daughter's golden-blond hair from her face. "You have such a unique way of looking at things. It is your hidden strength. Never forget that."

"Can I touch it?" the girl asked, her heart galloping wildly at the thought of feeling the aged gold surface beneath her fingertips.

But her mother shook her head. "Not yet, my dear. You're still too young. One day this heirloom will belong to you. But until then, I think it's best if you don't touch it. I wouldn't want you to accidentally break it."

"When?" the girl insisted, bouncing on her toes. "When will it be mine?"

Her mother smiled at her again. "When you're ready for the responsibility. When you're old enough to protect it, just as I have done all of these years."

Once Upon a Time

Hi, I'm Ally! You may know my
mother, Alice. She was known
for falling down rabbit holes,
talking to caterpillars, and
having tea with mad hatters.

Yup, I guess you could say she had a pretty curious
childhood. Me, on the other hand, I grew up in Auradon.
Nothing really exciting or curious usually happens around
here . . . which is too bad, because all my life I've
wanted to be a detective. I feel like I was born to solve
mysteries. I'm just so curious about everything. And
being a detective is the best way to satisfy your curiosity, except it's pretty hard to be a detective in a place
where there's no crime.

Although, recently, there have been some exciting changes around here. King Ben started letting villain kids (VKs) from the Isle of the Lost attend Auradon Prep! And let's just say, since then, interesting things have <u>finally</u> started to happen. First there was the mystery of the stolen wand at King Ben's coronation. Unfortunately, I wasn't there to solve it, but I totally <u>would</u> have solved it if I had been there. Then CJ, Captain Hook's daughter, snuck into Auradon Prep and started pulling all sorts of pranks around the school. And believe me, I was <u>this</u> close to unveiling her as the culprit before she . . . well, she kind of unveiled herself, so that was quite a bummer. And then there was the whole mess with Freddie's Shadow Cards, and . . . okay, so I didn't figure that one out, either, but I did help Freddie find Mama Odie's house, which was a pretty big deal. The point is, now that suspicious things are starting to happen around Auradon Prep, I am ready. Special Detective Ally is reporting for duty.

That's not a real title, by the way. I just made it up. But maybe someday it will be, if I can prove myself worthy of it.

I just have to find a good mystery to solve. . . .

Hold On a Minute

I think I might be onto something. . . .

Fairy Godmother's office was quite a mess. Every drawer and cabinet had been opened and emptied, and the large wooden desk was covered in a fine layer of white cake flour. Ally stood in the center of it all with a roll of clear plastic tape in one hand and a bag of flour in the other.

She was dusting for fingerprints.

And, as of yet, she'd been unsuccessful in lifting any.

But how was that even possible? How could the criminals have broken into Fairy Godmother's office, vandalized an entire wall with spray paint, and not left a single shred of evidence behind?

Ally had heard their mischievous laughter and the

rattling of the spray paint cans as they turned a corner in the Auradon Prep hallway, but by the time she had peeked into Fairy Godmother's office and noticed the wall had been defaced, the vandals were nowhere to be seen.

Ally stared at the spray-painted wall. It was the one facing Fairy Godmother's desk. On it the vandals had painted *Auradon Prep!* in giant colorful letters, and the rest of the wall had been decorated with all sorts of different figures and animals.

And they'd done it all, in the middle of the day, without getting caught.

It was shocking.

And it meant she'd have to rely on her detective instincts, plus whatever evidence she could gather from the crime scene, to solve the mystery—which was why she was here instead of at lunch in the banquet hall with the rest of the school, including Fairy Godmother herself.

Ally harrumphed. *Think,* she commanded herself. *Think harder.* She tapped her finger against her forehead. This always helped Ally do her best thinking. It was as though she could physically knock the thoughts into place.

What would the criminals have touched while they were here?

Her eyes scanned the spray-painted wall from top to bottom, taking in every inch of the graffiti. It covered the entire wall, all the way up to the ceiling. . . .

The ceiling! Ally thought with sudden realization. *Perhaps they touched the ceiling while they were painting the top half of the wall.*

Ally glanced around the office, locating a chair in the corner. She set down the tape and her bag of flour and dragged the chair over, positioning it just under the *P* in *Auradon Prep!*

Picking up her supplies once again, she stepped precariously onto the chair. She reached her hand into the bag and scooped out a handful of flour, tossing it up toward the ceiling. Unfortunately, only some of the flour made it onto the actual ceiling; the rest ended up falling in her face and making her cough.

After she'd finished expelling flour from her lungs, Ally tore off a piece of clear tape and reached up to affix it to the ceiling, right over the thin layer of white powder. She smoothed out the bubbles with her fingertip. Then she carefully peeled back the tape and stared at the sticky surface.

"Aha!" she said triumphantly. "Gotcha!"

On the back side of the tape was a fully formed, perfectly shaped, swirling fingerprint.

Now she just had to figure out *whose* fingerprint it was and she'd have solved the case. The only problem was there wasn't exactly a fingerprint database at Auradon Prep, or in all the United States of Auradon, as far as she knew. There wasn't even a police force. What was the point in a land with no villains?

But Ally would find a way. Even if she had to secretly fingerprint every single person in the school, she would figure out how to match the print with one of the culprits responsible for this outrageous act of school vandalism.

"Special Detective Ally cracks yet another Auradon mystery," she announced proudly, trying to make her posh English accent sound more like that of an American newscaster.

Proud of her newfound evidence, Ally carefully affixed the piece of tape to a sheet of notepaper from Fairy Godmother's desk, put it in the pocket of her dress, and started to step down from the chair. But just then, a bit of flour fell from the ceiling and got into her eye, momentarily blinding her. As she rubbed at her eye, she felt the chair beneath her wobble.

"Oh, crumbs," Ally swore as she tried to right herself. But it was a lost cause. Ally was the first to admit her coordination wasn't the greatest. She was constantly falling. It was a genetic trait that ran in the family. Once your mother falls down a rabbit hole, perhaps your balance is forever doomed.

Ally flailed. The chair tipped and down she fell, the bag slipping from her hands. Flour rained down all over Fairy Godmother's office like powdery snow.

Ally landed on her bottom with a *thump*. She was about to stand up, dust herself off, and quickly try to clean up the mess, but she suddenly realized she wasn't alone.

The door to the office had opened and Fairy Godmother herself was now standing in the doorway, looking gobsmacked.

JUST A SEC

*I thought Fairy Godmother would
appreciate my efforts. But she
seemed a little . . . displeased.*

The headmistress of the school let out an enormous gasp at the sight of what had become of her office.

"Ally!" she cried out, her hand covering her mouth. "What happened here? Are you all right?"

Ally stood and dusted off her blue-and-white dress, which had gotten a bit rumpled (not to mention powdery) in the fall. "You'll be happy to know I have everything under control, Fairy Godmother," Ally said confidently. "The vandals will be caught and brought to justice."

"Vandals?" Fairy Godmother repeated. She sounded

confused. Ally reckoned she simply hadn't yet noticed the graffitied wall in front of her. She was probably still too hung up on the chaotic state of her office. It did quite resemble an explosion in a scone factory.

"Yes," Ally said, gesturing dramatically toward the wall. "What we have here is an obvious case of student vandalism, but I now have, in my possession, the evidence we need to track down the persons responsible."

Fairy Godmother followed Ally's pointed fingertip toward the spray-painted wall. She seemed to be thinking long and hard about something before comprehension finally settled on her face. Ally expected her to be outraged, just as Ally had been when she first stepped into the office and saw the ghastly sight. But the only expression Ally could read on Fairy Godmother's face was disappointment.

The headmistress let out a weary sigh and walked behind her desk. She brushed the flour off her chair with a dainty flick and took a seat. "Ally," she said in a stern voice that Ally didn't like one bit. "Sit down, please."

Ally did as she was told, but she was confused. Why wasn't Fairy Godmother more upset about this?

Why wasn't she eager to hear about Ally's evidence? They were wasting precious time! They should be narrowing down a list of suspects, questioning potential witnesses. They needed to search every student's dorm room for empty spray cans! They needed to—

"That is not vandalism," Fairy Godmother spoke very clearly. "That was Mal, Lonnie, and Jay."

Ally's eyes grew wide as crumpets. "You *know* who did it?"

"I do," Fairy Godmother said, "because I *asked* them to."

Now Ally was just befuddled. Her eyes narrowed into tiny slits. "I don't understand. Why would you *ask* someone to vandalize your office?"

"I asked them to *decorate* my office," Fairy Godmother explained with a sigh, "with this lovely mural. The walls in here are far too boring. I wanted a pop of color. So I told them to come before lunch and paint the wall."

Ally's mouth fell open. She tried to speak but it was as though her lips had forgotten how to form words.

"So, you see," the headmistress went on, "there

was no crime committed here. Apart from the possible crime of your covering my office with what seems to be"—Fairy Godmother dipped her fingertip in the white powder that covered her desk and touched it to her tongue—"flour?"

"It's *cake* flour," Ally corrected her, grumbling.

"Mmm hmmm," mused Fairy Godmother, and Ally was convinced she was about to scold her. Students weren't allowed to enter Fairy Godmother's office when she wasn't there. Ally had very clearly broken the rules. But she'd *thought* these were extenuating circumstances. She'd *thought* it was warranted. Plus, even though she was an Auradon kid (AK), Ally had never been a big fan of rules. Unlike her best friend, Jane, who, ever since she'd stolen Fairy Godmother's wand and gotten in trouble, seemed to be following the rules a little *too* much. Ally always felt as though rules were too stringent; they usually didn't allow for special circumstances, which Ally could almost *always* find.

But to Ally's surprise, Fairy Godmother *didn't* scold or reprimand her. She simply folded her hands in her lap and asked in a kind voice, "Ally, did you ever stop to think that maybe the 'vandals,' as you called them, were actually supposed to be here? Instead of immediately jumping to the worst-case scenario?"

"No," Ally replied tightly. "I relied on my instincts. Just like all good detectives do. And my instincts were telling me a crime had been committed."

Fairy Godmother offered her an unexpected smile. "It's true, good detectives *do* rely on their instincts. But they also know when to slow down, read the clues, and think things through logically."

Logically?

Ally didn't like that word. It was a boring word for boring people. Who needed logic and reason when you had smarts and hunches like she had?

"Detectives are methodical about their investigations," Fairy Godmother went on. "They analyze the evidence before coming to conclusions."

Ally had stopped listening. She was too busy trying to come up with an anagram for the word *logically*. That's what she did when she was bored, or nervous, or scared. She took words she didn't like and rearranged the letters to make the words more interesting.

Hmmm. Logically, Ally thought.

Gilly coal?

Lilac logy?

Cagily LOL?

"Do you agree?" Fairy Godmother was saying. "Ally?"

Ally blinked and focused back on the headmistress. "What?"

Fairy Godmother sighed. "I said, you seem to be jumping to a lot of incorrect conclusions recently. Perhaps the next time you believe a crime has been committed, you should come to me first, instead of taking matters into your own hands. How does that sound?"

Ally sighed in surrender and then nodded. "Fine."

Fairy Godmother beamed. "Excellent. I'm glad we understand each other. So, how are the preparations going for the Spirit Weekend Reception? Do you have everything ready for the food table?"

But Ally didn't answer. She was off in her own thoughts again, letters swimming through her mind like fish in a tank.

"Ally?" Fairy Godmother prompted. Then a second later, *"Ally?"*

"That's it!" Ally jumped from her chair.

Fairy Godmother startled. "*What's* it?"

"Ally logic!" she said, feeling mighty proud of herself. It was a ridiculously simple rearrangement of the letters, but it was without a doubt the best possible anagram for the word *logically*.

Well done, she silently commended herself.

"What is Ally logic?" Fairy Godmother asked, clearly not following.

Ally grinned. "It means logic with a twist!"

And with that, she skipped out of the headmistress's office, leaving Fairy Godmother too bewildered to say anything else.

DIAL IT BACK

So maybe I jumped to a conclusion back
there. It happens. Next time, I'll
wait for the mystery to come to me.

After she left Fairy Godmother's office, Ally headed
to the banquet hall to grab something quick to eat.
Since she'd missed lunch, she was starving. All of Ally's
friends were already rushing off to prepare for Spirit
Weekend, which officially started that afternoon at the
big reception in the royal hall. Spirit Weekend was a
yearly tradition at Auradon Prep, held to rally excitement for the first big tourney game of the season. This
year, Auradon Prep was facing off against its biggest
rival, the Never Land Crocs, and Spirit Weekend was
shaping up to be a major event.

Evie, Evil Queen's daughter, hurried past Ally, mentioning something about putting the finishing touches on a new dress as she darted out of the banquet hall. Jane and Audrey set off for the carnival grounds to get ready for the banner-painting party scheduled for later that evening, which Audrey was in charge of. And Mal disappeared to the tourney field to finish prepping for the next day's big concert. She had a secret: as a surprise for Ben, she had gotten his favorite band, Talking Dragons, to play the concert that happened at the end of Spirit Weekend. Mal hadn't been able to stop talking to her friends about it since she'd booked the band. "I can't wait to see the look on his face when they take the stage," Mal kept saying. "He's going to totally flip out."

Ally had work to do, too. She had volunteered to cater the reception and there was still much to do to get ready. So she gobbled down a quick sandwich and started off for the tea shop.

As she walked through Auradon Prep's beautifully landscaped campus, Ally told herself not to be deterred by what had happened in Fairy Godmother's office earlier. So she'd jumped to the wrong conclusion. So what? It was a small setback. A minor stumbling block. She wasn't giving up. She would find her mystery to solve, she was sure of it.

But for some reason, she couldn't shake what Fairy Godmother had said to her just moments before: *You seem to be jumping to a lot of incorrect conclusions recently.*

Ally had to admit the headmistress was just a *tad* right. Some of the so-called mysteries that Ally had tried to solve in the past few weeks had been a little ridiculous. Like, for example, the mystery of the broken teacup at her mother's tea shop the previous week. Ally had suspected foul play, that someone had broken in to rob the place, but it turned out Evie had just accidentally dropped it on her last visit. She'd apologized to Ally's mother and everything. Then there was the mystery of the kidnapped teacher. At least Ally had *believed* he'd been kidnapped. But Fairy Godmother had revealed a few hours later that he was simply on vacation. And then, of course, who could forget the case of the stolen jacket? She'd seen Lonnie wearing Jordan's shimmery gold jacket and *assumed* Lonnie had pilfered it. It turned out, however, that Jordan had just *lent* the jacket to Lonnie. Which, in hindsight, *did* seem like the obvious explanation.

The problem was Ally saw things differently. She always had. Her mother told her it was her biggest strength; lately it just seemed to be getting her in trouble. But Ally had no choice. She had to follow her instincts—it was the only way she knew how to be.

"Hey!" a deep male voice said, and suddenly there was a hand waving in front of Ally's face. Ally hadn't even realized that she'd stopped walking and was just standing in the middle of the path, staring off into space.

She blinked and focused on the person in front of her. It was Jay, Jafar's son. He was carrying two cans of blue spray paint, and Ally suddenly remembered something else Fairy Godmother had said: *I asked them to* decorate *my office.*

"Ally?" Jay said, bending down so he could make eye contact with her.

"Oh, hi, Jay," Ally said absently.

Jay snickered. "Are you off in Ally Land again?"

Ally squinted. "Huh?"

"You are. I thought so."

"What's Ally Land?"

Jay looked somewhat sheepish. "Just a little name we came up with to explain what happens when you

22

go all dreamy-eyed like that. We say you're in Ally Land." He shrugged. "I imagine it's kind of like your own little version of Wonderland."

Ally Land? Ally thought, her mind immediately trying to pinpoint the best anagram.

All and Ly
La La Lynd
Land, y'all!

Jay must have mistaken Ally's pensiveness for offense, because he quickly added, "Don't worry. It's not a bad thing. Trust me, there are days that I'd love to visit Ally Land. Based on your expression, it seems like a really awesome place!"

"Of course it is!" Ally chirped. But she wasn't really listening to what Jay was saying. She was already back to thinking about the mysteries that weren't really mysteries: the broken teacup and the teacher and the spray-painted wall. Was it really her fault that they hadn't actually been crimes?

Jay chuckled. "Okay, well, I better get this paint to the carnival grounds before Audrey totally loses it. She's setting up for the banner-making party tonight and she's all sorts of stressed. If these banners don't look perfect, I don't even want to know what she'll

do. See you at the reception later. I'm really looking forward to that carrot cake you baked!" Then he
waved and took off down the path.

Ally sighed and kept walking. When she arrived a
few minutes later at Mad for Tea, the tea shop she ran
with her mother, she immediately filled a kettle with
water and lit the burner. A nice hot cup of tea would
make her feel better. It always did. When she was a
little girl, her mum used to make tea for her whenever
she was having a tough day, and it had always cheered
her up.

As Ally waited for the kettle to boil, she turned
and surveyed the empty tea shop. All of the teacups and saucers were in their rightful places on the
shelves. The tea leaves were all tucked neatly into
their tins. Even the three-tiered carrot cake Ally had
baked for the party was still sitting untouched on its
shining silver platter on the counter. Everything was
peaceful and quiet—just like the rest of Auradon.

Ally slumped as she considered the possibility that
there might be no need for a detective in Auradon.
Maybe there were just no real mysteries to be solved.

Then Ally took a step backward and her foot
went straight through the floor.

A Momentary Surprise

Don't worry. I quickly recovered
from the shock of stepping
through the floor. It was more
exciting than scary, actually.

Ally's foot had completely disappeared under the floor-boards of the tea shop. All she could see was her knee, which was now exposed due to the rip in her blue-and-white striped tights, revealing a scrape on her skin.

"Oh, boiling teakettles! What's this?" Ally carefully pulled her leg out of the foot-sized hole she'd made in the floor and bent down to look into it. Dino, her red-and-white striped cat, slunk over and stared into the gap with her. They exchanged curious glances.

The wooden board, which had once been attached

to the rest of the floor, was lying in two pieces at the bottom of the hole. Ally reached down to pick up one of the pieces and examine it. It was warped and discolored. She showed Dino, as if asking the cat for his assessment.

Dino meowed.

Ally nodded. "That was my conclusion, too. This must have been leftover damage from the flood."

A few months before, Ally had thrown a party in the tea shop. It was a fund-raiser for her a capella group, the Auradonnas. But the party had been a little *too* successful, and so many people had shown up that she'd had to move all the furniture into the back storage closet to make room for everyone. What Ally hadn't known at the time was that the furniture was leaning against a water pipe, which eventually burst and flooded the whole tea shop. Apparently, some of the floorboards had been damaged.

Ally sighed. She would have to call someone to fix this. But she couldn't worry about that now. She had lots to do to set up for the Spirit Weekend Reception.

Ally was about to drop the broken board back into the hole when she noticed something else down there. It was round and kind of a dull gold color. Ally slid her hand into the hole and attempted to reach the item, but her arm wasn't quite long enough. She maneuvered onto her belly and extended her arm farther. Her hand touched something cool and metallic; it felt like a chain. She hooked her fingertip through it and slowly lifted the object.

Ally gasped when she saw what was dangling from the end of her finger.

"Meow!" said Dino excitedly.

"Yes!" Ally replied. "It's Mum's old pocket watch!" The watch swung back and forth on the chain, and both Ally's and Dino's eyes flicked from side to side, following it.

"Meow?" Dino asked.

"Mum must have hidden it here," Ally explained. She remembered the pocket watch from when she was a little girl. Her mother had always told her she wasn't old enough to touch it yet because she might accidentally break it.

But she was certainly old enough now!

With a giddy yip, Ally jumped to her feet. But she must have moved too fast, because the watch slipped from her fingertip and started to plummet back down into the hole.

"Meow!" Dino cried at the same time Ally cried "No!"

Ally scrambled to catch the watch, but it bounced off her open palm and for a moment seemed to be flying through the air in slow motion, the long chain drifting behind like it was caught in an invisible breeze. Dino clamored to get out of the way as Ally dove toward it with her hands outstretched, feeling like a tourney player trying to block a goal.

Unfortunately, she'd never been that good of a tourney player, and the watch tumbled to the ground just out of her reach.

"Oh, dear!" Ally said, and she scrambled forward to grab it. She immediately brought the pocket watch to her ear, listening anxiously for the faint *tick tick tick* of the second hand. When she was little she'd thought it was the watch's heartbeat. And everyone knows what happens when a heartbeat stops.

Ally listened and waited, her heart in her throat. She pressed the clock harder against her ear. Then, finally, she heard it.

Tick. Tick. Tick.

She breathed a sigh of relief. "It's still alive. Thank

goodness. That was a close one. Let's not tell Mum about that."

With a meow, Dino swore himself to secrecy.

Ally remembered her mother, Alice, telling her stories about her time in Wonderland, where she'd met all sorts of fun and interesting people and animals. Her mum had made friends with a caterpillar who could talk, a cat who could disappear, and even a rabbit who wore a waistcoat and had a pocket watch very similar to this one.

Ally wondered if this watch had possibly come from Wonderland. Or perhaps it was made in Tweedleton. That was a town on the other side of Auradon where many of her mother's Wonderland friends had retired. Ally had never been there, but her mum had talked about it a few times. Her mother told Ally she didn't like going to Tweedleton.

"It's a very curious place," Alice had once explained. "A little too curious for my taste." Ally had always wanted to visit so she could get a taste of what Wonderland might have been like, but her mother had refused to take her whenever she'd asked. "That silly town does my head in," Alice said.

Now Ally cradled the watch to her chest, carefully stood up, and carried it over to the tea shop counter. She set it down, excited to finally be able to examine it for the first time. The pocket watch was lovely. Ally adored the old look and feel of it. Most things in Auradon looked shiny and new, so this seemed extra special. It was made of gold that had long before lost its luster, and the numbers on the clock face were slightly faded. Not that Ally could see them very well, since the glass was all smudged.

"I think I'll clean it," Ally said to herself, turning and marching over to the cupboard where her mum kept the cleaning supplies. Ally had been working at the tea shop since she was a child. Her mother had always let her help with various chores, like baking scones and scrubbing cake tins and sorting tea leaves. Ally enjoyed it. It made her feel closer to her mother.

She pulled out a cloth and some cleaning spray and spritzed the face of the watch.

"Mum is going to be so proud of me," Ally told Dino as she rubbed gently on the glass. "Not only did I find the watch, I'm also cleaning it up for her! And *not* breaking it."

Ally pulled the cloth back and admired her work. "Much better. I can't wait to show it to Jane!"

Dino jumped on the counter and tilted his head to examine the watch. "Meow," he said approvingly.

"Thank you," Ally said. "I agree. It still looks old but at least you can see through the glass now."

Ally flipped the watch over to study the back, and that was when she noticed something engraved on the gold surface. "Look, Dino, there's writing here."

She squinted to try to read it but there was much too much dirt to be able to make out any of the letters. Ally grabbed the cleaner and gave the back side a spritz. As she wiped away the grime, she started to make out the words.

MR WEIDEN

Ally looked to Dino. "Mr. Weiden? Now who do you suppose *that* could be?"

"Meow?" Dino guessed.

Ally smiled and gave him a pat. "You're so smart. Of course! It must be the watchmaker. They always engrave their names onto the watch, don't they? I imagine he lives in Tweedleton with some of Mum's old friends."

Just then, the water in the teakettle on the burner came to a boil, letting out a sharp screeching whistle that caused Ally to jump. She'd completely forgotten about her tea! And apparently, so had Dino, because he hissed in surprise and leapt straight into the air, clawing furiously at nothing.

"Dino!" Ally reprimanded. "Calm down!"

But it was no use. The cat was freaked out. And just as he dropped past the counter, his paw accidentally snagged the chain of the pocket watch, bringing it crashing to the floor with a horrifying *whack*.

IN A SPLIT SECOND

It happened so quickly. And I
was being so careful. I felt like
I might cry—the kind of crying
that fills a room with tears.

"Oh, you clumsy, clumsy kitty! Now look what you've done!"

Ally bent down to pick up the fallen watch. It was definitely broken now. The glass face was shattered. Ally held the remnants of the heirloom up to her ear again, waiting anxiously for the *tick tick tick* of the second hand.

This time, however, there was nothing but silence.

She shook the watch and listened again.

But the only heartbeat she could hear was her own,

thudding wildly in her chest. What was she going to do? How would she tell her mother? Her mother would be so disappointed with her!

"Please," she implored the clock. "Please, don't be dead."

But the watch didn't move. The hands were frozen at 1:30 p.m.

It was already 1:30 p.m.?

Ally jolted to attention. She had completely lost track of time. The Spirit Weekend kickoff party started in a half hour and she still had to bring the cake to the royal hall *and* set up the rest of the food table.

"Mad hatters!" she cried. "I'm late!"

She shoved the broken watch into the pocket of her dress, vowing to figure out how to fix it later. There had to be a watchmaker nearby who could revive the watch's heart. Maybe she would have a look for that Mr. Weiden fellow.

But she would deal with that another time. For now, she had a cake to contend with. Ally carefully picked up the giant three-tiered carrot cake she'd baked the night before and began to make her way toward the royal hall. But it was frustrating how slowly she had to walk to make sure the cake didn't topple over.

Ally was not used to doing *anything* slowly. She was always eager to race into everything she did. Like how she'd volunteered to cater the Spirit Weekend Reception. As soon as Fairy Godmother had announced it was happening, Ally's hand shot straight into the air. "Mad for Tea can supply the food!" she'd offered before she could even think about how much work that would entail. But by the time she'd had a moment to second-guess her offer, everyone was cheering and Fairy Godmother was beaming and it was too late.

Along the way to the royal hall, Ally heard several Auradon Prep students shout things like "Nice cake, Ally!" "Looks delicious, Ally!" "Can't wait to get my hands on that!" But unfortunately, Ally had no idea *who* was saying any of it, because the cake was so tall she couldn't see over the top. So she just called back "Thanks!" to everyone she heard and kept walking.

By the time Ally made it through the grand front doors of the royal hall and was able to set the cake down on the food table, she was totally exhausted and out of breath. But she knew she didn't have much time for rest. The party was going to start soon and she still had so much to do to prepare!

For the next twenty minutes, Ally was like a bee that had consumed too much caffeinated tea. She buzzed around the royal hall, filling teapots, arranging sandwiches on trays, and making sure every last detail was perfect.

Moments before the guests arrived, Ally took a step back to admire her work. She had to admit, the food table looked magnificent with its towering trays of freshly baked cookies and scones, tiny tea sandwiches perfectly cut into triangles, and hot pots of tea in every flavor from chamomile to peppermint to Darjeeling. And in the center of it all, her masterpiece: the three-tiered carrot cake complete with white cream cheese frosting and decorated for Spirit Weekend in the Auradon Prep signature blue and gold.

She beamed, took her phone out of her pocket, and snapped a photo.

"Well done," she commended herself as she studied the photo, noticing how the light shone perfectly on the cake's sparkling silver platter. But she frowned at the screen when she noticed something was missing.

"Oh, swizzle sticks!" Ally swore. "I forgot the clotted cream for the scones!"

She checked the time on her phone. The reception was scheduled to start in two minutes! She'd have to hurry. Ally pocketed her phone and took off through the front door, running at a full sprint to the tea shop. She grabbed the clotted cream from the refrigerator and doubled back to the royal hall. But even though she ran at top speed, the reception had already started by the time Ally returned. Lonnie was deejaying from the stage and the room was packed with people. As Ally tried to make her way through the crowd to set down the bowl of cream she was holding, she kept getting intercepted by people who stopped her to compliment the spread.

"Looks amazing!" Fairy Godmother told her, patting her on the back. "Well done, Ally."

"Fairies couldn't even have done a better job," Audrey praised.

"Wicked," Evie commended.

"I wish I had your culinary skills," Mal said. "I tried to bake cookies once. Total failure."

In fact, the only person Ally didn't see on the way to the food table was her best friend, Jane. Ally glanced around the room before finally spotting Jane in the center of a small circle of girls who all appeared to be admiring something on Jane's wrist.

"It's just beautiful!" one girl cooed.

"I've never seen anything like it," another one said.

Jane was beaming. Ally had never seen a smile so big on her face. She wondered what they were all fussing over. Ally took a few steps closer and stood on her tiptoes to see over the heads in the crowd. She caught a flash of a gorgeous gold watch encrusted with tiny diamonds on Jane's wrist.

"I can't believe your mom let you borrow it," one of the admirers said.

"I know!" Jane squealed. "I've been asking my mom to borrow it for years, but she always said I wasn't old enough. It *is*, after all, a family heirloom. So it's *very* valuable."

For a moment, Ally thought about the broken pocket watch still sitting in the pocket of her dress. It was also a valuable family heirloom. And her mum had always said *she* was too young to have it, too. Then she had broken it, not five minutes after finding it. The guilt and shame warmed Ally's face. She had been so excited to find the watch and show Jane, but now she actually just wanted to forget about it.

Ally turned away, focusing on her task. She continued toward the food table to deliver the clotted cream, which was still cradled in her hands.

"These chocolate scones are delicious!" Cruella De Vil's son, Carlos, mumbled through a mouthful of crumbs.

"The best I've ever tasted!" Chad Charming agreed, holding up a half-eaten scone as Ally passed by.

Ally couldn't help beaming at all the praise. Who cared about broken pocket watches and failed mysteries? Maybe she should just forget about being a detective and work in the tea shop for the rest of her life. She was clearly good at it. Besides, she was starting to come to the sad realization that there really *was* no crime in Auradon.

"Way to go with that food table," someone said, and Ally turned around to see Jay standing there.

Ally smiled at him. "Thanks."

Jay looked pensive for a second. He scratched his chin like he was trying to decide whether or not to say something.

"What is it?" Ally asked.

Jay shrugged. "No biggie. But, um . . . I thought you said something about baking a carrot cake. I've been thinking about it all day. I love the cream cheese frosting, you know?" Then he quickly added. "But the cookies are delicious, too!"

Ally frowned in confusion. "What are you talking about? I *did* make the cake."

"You did?"

Ally snorted with laughter. "Of course, silly. How could you miss it? It's right over—" But when she turned around to point out the giant three-tiered white-frosted cake sitting tall in the center of the food spread, she suddenly couldn't speak. Her body went still as her eyes darted anxiously back and forth over the length over the table.

The cake! The one Ally had spent hours baking, frosting, and decorating, not to mention *carrying* all the way to the royal hall.

It was gone.

DESSERTS FOR DAYS

Yes, it's true, I had made more
desserts and baked goods than
anyone could possibly eat. But the
cake—my pastry de résistance—
was the crown jewel of the
display. And it wasn't there!

Ally ran to the table, her eyes roving over the various snacks and treats. Everything else was there—the cookies, the sandwiches, the scones—but now there was a giant empty space in the center of the table.

Ally's eyes nearly popped out of her head. She hastily set down her bowl of clotted cream, yanked her phone out of her pocket, and pulled up the photo she had taken right before the guests started to arrive.

There was definitely a cake in the picture. She wasn't imagining things.

Where could it have gone? Ally thought, glancing around. She looked behind the table. She looked on either side of the table. But it wasn't until she lifted up the white linen tablecloth and looked *beneath* the table that she understood what had happened.

Ally let out a shriek of surprise.

There, on the floor under the food table, was a silver platter. The *same* silver platter Ally had used to carry and display the cake. Except now, all that was on it was a scattering of brown crumbs and smudges of white frosting.

Someone ate my cake? Ally thought with horror as she pulled the platter out from under the table and gaped at it.

Someone had definitely eaten the cake. But not just *eaten* it. Gobbled it. *Devoured* it.

But how could that have happened? Ally wondered in frustration. *I was here the whole time—*

She stopped the thought in its tracks as she glanced down at the bowl of clotted cream on the table in front of her.

No. I wasn't here the whole time. I ran back to the tea shop to get the cream. Someone must have eaten the cake while I was gone.

But who?

She suddenly had a flash of a memory. People calling out to her as she was walking over with the cake:

Nice cake, Ally!

Looks delicious, Ally!

Can't wait to get my hands on that!

Can't wait to get my hands on that? That was certainly a peculiar thing to say, wasn't it? Those sounded like the words of a cake thief.

The problem was Ally had no idea *who* had said those words, because the giant towering cake had been blocking her view. It was definitely a girl's voice, but it was only vaguely familiar.

Ally scanned the room, trying to focus on each individual female face. But she soon came to the conclusion that it could have been any one of those girls who'd said the words to her.

If the person who said it was even a suspect.

Suspect. Ally repeated the word in her mind,

immediately mixing up the letters to try to find an anagram. But this time, she didn't need one. The word itself was exciting enough.

Suspect.

A real suspect in a real case!

It appeared Ally had finally found her mystery.

Stop. Everything.

I knew what had happened:
there had been a cake-napping.
And I was on the case.

"Everybody freeze!" Ally cried out where she stood. "Nobody move."

The voices in the room faded until the only sound was the music blasting from Lonnie's DJ equipment.

Time to take control of the situation, Ally thought.

"Lonnie!" she called. "Cut the music."

Lonnie, looking worried, reached for her controls, muting the sound.

Ally turned to Jay, who was still standing nearby. "Block the front entrance. Make sure no one gets out of here unquestioned."

Jay appeared confused by the directive but then seemed to understand and darted over to the entrance. He stood in front of it, arms crossed, legs rigid, looking mighty pleased with his tough exterior.

Let the mystery of the gobbled cake begin!

Ally climbed the steps of the stage and cast her gaze out over the entire room. "We have a problem," she called out, addressing the students who were all staring at her with blank expressions. No one seemed to know what was happening.

And that, Ally thought smugly, *is why* I'm *the detective here and not them. I notice things. I am observant.*

Ally surveyed the royal hall, drawing out her big announcement for as long as she could. She wanted to build suspense. She wanted everyone in the room to appreciate the severity of the situation.

"What's going on?" Mal called out, taking the role of unofficial spokesperson for the crowd, which had started to grow restless.

Ally cleared her throat. It was time to make her mark on Auradon history. In the loudest, most authoritative voice she could muster, she announced,

"We have a thief in our midst! Someone has eaten the entire Spirit Weekend Reception cake!"

She expected the room to erupt in gasps and boos and calls for justice. But everyone was silent. In fact, they all looked a little befuddled. Ally tried not to let her frustration show. "This is a very serious matter," she went on, hoping a little clarification might help. "There is a criminal among us! And this person must be caught and tried in the presence of His Royal Majesty King Ben!"

More confused looks from the crowd. And then a few people actually started *laughing*. No, not just a few people. *Everyone*. Everyone was laughing at her! Even people like Audrey and Freddie, who Ally thought were her friends.

Did they think this was a joke?

Ally fought the urge to stomp her foot at their ignorance. Why weren't they taking this seriously? Why couldn't they see the gravity of the situation?

"It was probably Chad Charming!" someone called from the group, and the room erupted into more laughter.

Ally could feel tears pricking her eyes. She quickly

blinked them away. She would not cry. Not here. Not now. She had a mystery to solve.

There's no room for emotion on a case! Ally reminded herself.

Mal and Evie approached the stage with cautious steps, as though they were explorers in the jungle and Ally was an injured wild animal that might strike.

"Ally," Mal said, her voice unusually gentle. "Don't you think you might be blowing this a *smidge* out of proportion? It's just a cake."

"A beautiful cake, no doubt," Evie added brightly.

"No," Ally said, and now she did stomp her foot. She couldn't help herself. "It's not just a cake! It's a crime! Someone gobbled up the entire thing!"

"Maybe they were just *really* hungry," Mal suggested, and Ally saw something flash on her face. It looked a lot like pity.

Ally's stomach clenched. She had to make Mal understand. She couldn't bear the thought of Mal feeling sorry of her. Mal couldn't *pity* her.

Ever since Ally had first met Mal, she'd been slightly in awe of her—and slightly terrified of her, too. Mal with her purple hair, her spiky clothes and calm confidence. She didn't let anything stand in her way. She faced her fears head-on. Ally, on the other hand, often let her fears get the better of her. She'd always wanted to be more like Mal. After all, detectives were supposed to be fearless. And it was that thought right there that caused Ally to stand up straighter, push her shoulders back, and regain her composure.

"It doesn't matter if they were hungry or not," Ally replied indignantly. "What matters is that a crime was committed and no one is fessing up. We need to take action right now. We need to line everyone up and search their hands and clothes for traces of carrot cake crumbs and white frosting. Whoever did this obviously can't get away with it."

Ally wished Mal and Evie would leap into action right that second, but they just turned and shared curious looks with each other. And that was when Ally noticed everyone in the room had gone back to what they were doing: talking, eating, and laughing.

No one was even paying attention to her anymore.

The music came back on the speakers, startling Ally. She turned to Lonnie with questioning eyes, but Lonnie just shrugged and said, "Sorry, Ally. Gotta keep the party going."

"Ally, why don't you come down from there so we can talk?" Mal suggested.

Begrudgingly, Ally obeyed and climbed down from the stage.

"What's this all about?" Mal asked, that pitying look suddenly back on her face. "This whole creating mysteries to solve."

Ally huffed. "I don't *create* mysteries to solve. I *see* crimes when they happen."

"But this is Auradon Prep," Evie argued, sounding genuinely confused. "There *are* no crimes here."

Ally snorted at this preposterous statement. "Of *course* there's crime at Auradon Prep."

"No, there's not," Mal said knowingly. "I'm a VK, so I can say that with authority."

"What about what happened with CJ?" Ally countered.

Mal bristled, probably remembering all the pranks CJ had pulled when she snuck into Auradon to be with her best friend, Freddie, who also happened to be Dr. Facilier's daughter. CJ hid out in Freddie's dorm room for a week, terrorizing the school with her pirate shenanigans. "Okay, I admit, CJ was *kind of* a criminal," Mal said. "But she's gone now. Off pillaging and plundering who knows where. Auradon Prep is safe from crime."

Ally opened her mouth to argue, but Mal cut her off. "Ally, do you think *maybe* you might be turning little things into big deals, just to have a case to solve?"

Ally was offended. Of course she wasn't doing that. She saw what she saw. The facts were the facts. She wasn't *changing* the facts just to create a mystery.

Was she?

Just then, Ally saw Jane making her way toward them, and Ally's hopes instantly lifted. Jane would understand. Jane would take her side and defend her. Jane was her best friend! Maybe Jane would even offer to help her find the cake thief.

"Jane," Ally said confidently. "You don't think I turn things into a bigger deal than they are, right? You don't think I *create* mysteries in my mind, do you?"

Jane refused to meet Ally's eyes as she fidgeted nervously with the ruffled hem of her blue-and-white polka-dotted dress. "W-w-well," she stammered in her soft voice, "I mean, it was kind of strange when you just assumed that teacher was kidnapped. Or when you assumed Lonnie had stolen Jordan's jacket. Or—"

"Those were misunderstandings," Ally interrupted, flustered. Her heart was starting to squeeze in her chest. It was one thing for Mal and Evie to doubt her, but Jane was her best friend. She was supposed to believe her no matter what! "This cake was here a few minutes ago. And now it's gone!" Ally pulled out her phone and showed Jane, Mal, and Evie the picture she had taken. "Don't you think that's strange?"

"Well, it was obviously very good if someone ate it that quickly," Jane said encouragingly. "I mean, if *you* baked it, how could it *not* be good?"

Ally could tell Jane was trying to comfort her using flattery. But Ally didn't need to be comforted—or flattered. She needed cooperation. She needed a best friend who took her side.

"Ally," Evie said, stepping forward to smooth Ally's long blond hair. "Why don't you enjoy the celebration? This is Spirit Weekend. It's supposed to be fun."

Ally snorted. *Fun?* Why was everyone just brushing this off like it was nothing?

Jane put her arm around Ally's shoulders in what Ally assumed was supposed to be a reassuring gesture. "I'm sure there's a logical explanation," Jane said.

Logical, Ally thought wearily. *Why does everyone around here only seem to care about what's logical?*

"Ally," Jane said sweetly, "don't worry about the cake. It'll be—"

Ally was certain Jane was about to tell her it would be okay, but she didn't wait around to hear that last part. She was already headed toward the back door of the royal hall. She had to get out of there. She was just going to go straight back to the tea shop and cuddle up in her favorite armchair with Dino, the only one on this campus who seemed to be on her side.

But just inches from the back door, Ally came to a screeching halt as her gaze was drawn to something on the floor. Something very, *very* suspicious.

Ally sniffled and brushed away her tears so she could see clearly.

In front of her was a small pile of what looked like light brown dirt.

No, not dirt . . .

Ally bent down and pressed her fingertip into the mysterious substance. First she smelled it. Then she tentatively licked the tip of her finger. The familiar sweet and spicy flavor danced on her tongue.

Just as she suspected.

Carrot cake crumbs.

Not a Minute to Waste

The cake thief left a trail!

Ally felt hopeful as she burst through the back door and out into the fresh afternoon air. She was determined to follow the cake crumbs until they led her to the perpetrator. She could just picture it now: diligently following the trail until she burst into a dorm room or supply closet or hidden lair, catching the thief red-handed with cream cheese frosting smeared across his or her face.

Oh, how the students would eat their words then! Everyone would have to acknowledge that Ally knew what she was doing. She could hear Mal now: *Ally, I'm sorry I didn't believe you. You were right all along. You're the best detective in all of—*

Ally froze. She stared down at her feet. Or more specifically, at the grass beneath her feet. It was bare. There were no cake crumbs. There was no trail. Just that small pile near the door, and then nothing.

"Oh, crumbs," she swore, before correcting herself. "I mean, *no* crumbs."

She giggled at her joke and immediately thought about telling it to Jane, who would certainly appreciate the humor. But then Ally remembered that she was upset at Jane for not believing her, and her laughter quickly fell away. She kicked the crumb-less grass in front of her.

This was a dead end.

Ally waited until everyone had gone to dinner before returning to the royal hall to clean up. She stood alone in the center of the large room, staring at the food table. All the trays of sandwiches, scones, and cookies had been picked over, leaving behind mostly crumbles, sprinkles, and a few stray pieces of lettuce. She frowned at the empty silver platter where her beautiful carrot cake once stood.

No one even got a chance to taste it.

Ally tried to calm her nerves by coming up with anagrams for *carrot cake*.

Cracker oat

A crate cork

Arc eat rock

She scoffed at that last one. "Well, that's just silly," she said to herself. "Arcs don't eat *rocks*."

Finally, she gave up and started to clear the table.

Thirty minutes later, after everything was clean, Ally left the royal hall and trudged back to her dorm room. On the way, she passed by the carnival grounds, where Audrey was ordering poor Jay around, telling him where to put the paints and how long to cut each piece of paper. They were obviously preparing for the banner-painting party, which started in less than an hour. The Spirit Weekend festivities would soon be in full swing.

Ally ducked her head so Audrey and Jay wouldn't notice her and kept walking.

Unfortunately, Ally's dorm room was right next to Jane's, which required her to pass by Jane's door on the way. And even *more* unfortunately, Ally could see as she rounded the corner, Jane's door was open.

Which meant she'd probably see Ally pass by and it would probably be awkward.

That was peculiar. It had never been awkward between the two girls before. They'd always been such good friends. The *best* of friends. They'd always been there for each other, even after that whole debacle with the magic wand Jane stole. Jane had a hard time after that: People looked at her differently. Ignored her in the hallways. Whispered things behind their hands. But not Ally. Ally had stuck by Jane's side the whole time. Just as a good friend should do.

But now it seemed like everyone was turning against Ally, and Jane was going right along with them. Accusing her of "creating" mysteries to solve. Thinking she was just a silly girl with her head in the clouds.

As Ally neared Jane's open door, she heard strange noises inside, along with some quiet murmuring. She told herself not to look. Not to pay it any attention. Just keep her eyes straight ahead and walk past the dorm room as fast as she could.

She didn't want to deal with Jane right then. She didn't even want to talk to her. She just wanted to sit alone in her dorm room and try to retrace the details of the day, in hopes that she could *maybe* come up with a clue she'd overlooked.

But as soon as she passed Jane's door, Ally heard a loud *bang*, and she jumped and turned instinctively, peering inside the room. Jane was standing in front of her dresser, just inside the door, with a huge scowl on her face. Ally watched her yank open a drawer, riffle around inside, and then shut it with another loud *bang*.

"Where *is* it?" Jane said, evidently to herself, because there was no one else in the room and she hadn't yet noticed Ally standing in the doorway. She was far too consumed by her search.

Ally could tell from the tone of her friend's voice that Jane was frustrated. It was the same tone she'd used a little while back when she couldn't find her Fighting Knights mascot costume. She'd searched everywhere before eventually finding out that CJ had stolen it.

See? Ally thought. *Crime in Auradon!*

Ally told herself to keep walking. Whatever Jane was looking for was no business of hers. But then Jane slammed another drawer closed and mumbled to herself, "I swear it was right here. It couldn't have just vanished into thin air."

Vanished into thin air?

Ally had always been a curious girl, and she usually let her curiosity get the better of her—another trait that seemed to run in the family. Curiosity, after all, was what had landed Ally's mother in Wonderland in the first place.

"What couldn't have vanished into thin air?" she asked, startling Jane, who jumped at the sound of Ally's voice and turned around.

"Oh, hi, Ally." She seemed frazzled and distracted. "Nothing. Just . . . um . . . well, it's my mother's watch. I seem to have misplaced it."

That definitely got Ally's attention. Her detective instincts were suddenly on high alert. Something was wrong here; she could feel it. Jane wasn't one to misplace things. She was pragmatic, organized, and logical. Basically all the things Ally was not.

"Misplaced it?" Ally repeated dubiously, stepping into the room. "Are you sure? Are you sure it wasn't, I don't know, maybe *stolen*?"

Jane turned to give Ally a confused look. "No, it wasn't stolen. Who would steal my mom's watch?"

Ally shrugged. "Perhaps someone with a preference for making an entire carrot cake disappear."

Jane chuckled. "Are you still on that silly cake mystery?"

The question stung, but Ally tried to push it to the back of her mind and soldier on. "What if someone *did* steal your mum's watch? What if the two things— my cake and *your* watch—are somehow connected?"

Jane shook her head like it was the most ridiculous thing she'd ever heard. "Of course it wasn't *stolen*. Who in Auradon would do something like that? And I don't see what a gobbled-up cake has to do with a watch. I'm sure I just put it somewhere and forgot. That explains it logically."

Ally harrumphed. There was that annoying word again. She much preferred its anagram: *Ally logic*. Logic with a twist.

"Well," Ally said, "where and when did you last see it?"

Jane's lips tugged into a frown. "Right here." She pointed to the top of her dresser. "I thought I put it right here after dinner."

"Then what did you do?" Ally asked, effortlessly slipping into detective mode.

Jane sighed. "I sat down at my desk to work on my History of Auradon homework. I thought I'd get a head start on it before the banner-painting party."

Ally eyed Jane's desk, noticing it faced *away* from the door. "So you were sitting here?" Ally asked, walking over to the desk and giving it a quick *tap tap tap* with her finger.

Jane nodded.

Ally glanced back at the dorm room door, which was conveniently situated just next to the dresser. "And that door was open at the time?"

Jane shrugged. "Yeah. Everyone keeps their dorm rooms open."

"Not the VKs," Ally pointed out.

Jane giggled. "Yeah, well, they're still a little paranoid."

"They really are, aren't they?" Ally laughed, too, and for a moment, she forgot all about why she was even there. It felt good to laugh with her best friend again.

But then Ally remembered her investigation and adjusted her expression. Good detectives didn't *socialize* on the job. They stayed serious and focused.

Ally cleared her throat. "So, just to recap, the

watch was on the dresser, your back was turned to the dresser when you were working, and the door was wide open. Meaning anyone could have reached in and swiped the watch."

Once again, Jane looked puzzled, as if Ally was speaking another language. "Huh?" Then, a moment later, comprehension seemed to dawn on Jane's face and she sighed in disappointment. "Ally, enough with the mystery stuff. I'm telling you no one stole the watch, I just forgot where I put it."

Ally could feel frustration boiling up inside her. Jane's watch had gone missing and she *still* didn't believe there was crime in Auradon?

"But you said," Ally argued, "that you put the watch on the dresser."

"I said I *think* I put it there. But I could be wrong. I probably put it somewhere else. I just need to keep looking."

"Did you *hear* anything unusual while you were doing your homework?" Ally asked. If she could find the person who stole the watch, she could finally prove to Jane (and everyone) that she was right: that crime existed in Auradon, and so did the need for a good detective. She could finally get everyone to take her seriously. Maybe the cake wasn't a big deal to them, but a missing valuable family heirloom? That should get everyone's attention!

"Ally," Jane started to protest.

"Just answer the question, please," Ally pressed. "Did you or did you not hear anything unusual while you were doing your homework?"

She knew she was badgering Jane, but sometimes that was what good detectives had to do to get information out of people.

"No," Jane replied. "I didn't hear anything unusual, because—"

Ally was certain Jane was about to say, yet again, "because there's no crime in Auradon," but curiously, she never finished her sentence. Jane's eyes kind of clouded over and she bit her lower lip, like she was lost in thought.

"What?" Ally urged.

"Nothing," Jane muttered. "I . . ." She shook her head. "Nothing."

But Ally didn't believe her. She knew Jane had suddenly remembered something. She could sense it. "What?" she asked again. "Tell me."

"I'm sure it was nothing," Jane was quick to say.

"It's just, I do remember hearing a weird kind of pattering noise."

Pattering noise, Ally echoed in her mind, taking mental note of the clue.

Getting a bit more into the details, Jane went on, "Like someone taking really tiny steps. Almost more like a tapping than a step."

Tiptoeing, Ally immediately thought with excitement. *Someone was sneaking through the hallway.*

"I wanted to see what it was," Jane continued, "but when I turned around, there was nothing there."

"Are you sure? You didn't see *anything* when you turned around?"

Jane bit her lip again, thinking. Then she looked at Ally, eyes wide. "Well, there was this shadow."

"A shadow?" Ally repeated.

"Yeah. But I only saw it for a moment and then it was gone."

Ally was even more suspicious. "Do you remember anything specific about the shadow? Like was it tall or short or large or small or—"

Jane paused. "But it could have just been someone coming back from dinner."

"What if it wasn't? What if it was the person who

took your watch? So, please, just tell me what the shadow looked like."

Jane thought about it for a moment. "Okay. Well, it had a strange protrusion on its head."

Ally squinted. "A protrusion? What do you mean?"

"The shadow's head was strangely shaped. Like the person had a very high ponytail or something."

"A ponytail!" Ally repeated eagerly, tapping her forehead. "That's good. That's *very* good. That definitely narrows down the list of suspects."

"Yes, it does," Jane said, and Ally heard something peculiar in Jane's voice.

When she refocused on Jane she saw that Jane was staring directly at Ally's hair. Ally touched the top of her head before remembering that *she*, herself, was wearing her hair in a very high ponytail, just as she normally did.

Jane's eyes widened in horror. "Ally, did *you* steal my mom's watch?"

Ally was shocked. "*What?* No! Of course not! Why would I steal your mum's watch?"

Jane suddenly burst into laughter. "Ally! I was kidding! Of course I don't think you stole my mom's watch. Even though you've been a little desperate lately for a mystery, I don't think you'd go that far!"

"Not funny!" Ally cried.

"You're right. I'm sorry." Jane pulled her phone out of her pocket and checked the time. "But the banner-painting party starts soon. We should head down to the carnival grounds and see if Audrey needs any help getting ready."

Ally shook her head at her friend. "Banner painting will have to wait. We need to stay focused if we're going to figure this mystery out! Are you on board or what?"

"Well," Jane began, sounding unsure.

"Look. If I'm wrong, no harm done. But if I'm right, and there *is* a bigger mystery here, then we'll find your mum's watch. So really, what do you have to lose?"

Jane thought about that for a moment before finally replying, "Okay. Where do we start?"

Full Speed Ahead

We have a clue. It may just be a ponytail, but I know we're just a hair away from solving this. Hahaha!

Ally peeked her head out of Jane's room, and when she saw no one was in the hallway, she slowly and quietly shut the door so the two of them could be alone and unheard.

"Okay, think," she told Jane. "Who in this school wears their hair in a high ponytail? Besides me, obviously."

Jane pressed her lips together and squinted her eyes, trying to picture all the girls at Auradon Prep. Ally sat down on the edge of the bed and tapped her finger against her forehead, trying to focus her thoughts.

"What we really need is some kind of registry with everyone's picture in it so we can quickly skim through all the students in the school and check for ponytails," Jane mused.

That's when the idea hit her, and Ally immediately shot to her feet. "InstaRoyal!" she exclaimed. She pulled her phone out of her pocket and clicked on the InstaRoyal app. Everyone at Auradon Prep had a profile on InstaRoyal. All she had to do was narrow down a list of girls who had ponytails and go from there.

"Of course!" Jane shouted, excited.

Ally instantly got pumped about the plan. It sounded like a very detective-like thing to do. And maybe even, dare she say it, *logical*.

As she and Jane perused the app, the first profile to appear was Mal's.

"Mal always wears her hair down, straight, and short," Jane noted.

"Not to mention Mal has no motive. Plus, she's been way too busy lately setting up the surprise Talking Dragons concert for Ben. She's had no time to steal desserts or watches," Ally confirmed.

Ally swiped to the next profile and studied the picture of Lonnie.

"Lonnie could have stolen the cake when she came in to set up her DJ equipment," Ally noted suspiciously.

"But she doesn't fit the description of the shadow," Jane reminded her, pointing at Lonnie's hair, which was loosely braided down her back in the photo, the same way she always wore it.

Ally swiped again. Evie's profile picture appeared next. But she usually wore her hair down, as well. Ally and Jane quickly ruled her out and swiped to the next profile, which was Audrey's. Jane acknowledged that although Audrey could be a pain sometimes, she wasn't likely a thief. Plus she never wore her hair up, and she had an alibi.

"Yes, and on my way back to the dorm, I saw Audrey setting up for the banner-painting party at the carnival grounds. So there was no way she could have stolen the watch," Ally concluded.

She moved on to the next profile.

"Jordan!" Ally yelled as soon as the picture of the Genie's daughter came onto her screen. "Jordan *always* wears her hair in a high ponytail, with that gold cuff."

Jane shook her head. "Jordan isn't even here this weekend. She's visiting her dad, remember?"

"Right." Ally sighed and swiped again, her finger freezing as soon as the next profile appeared.

Frolicking fruitcakes!

Ally's eyes widened as she stared at the picture on her phone screen. She couldn't believe it. The girl in the photo wore a small hat perched atop her head.

Jane was wrong, Ally realized with astonishment. "Jane!" she shouted at her friend in excitement. "It wasn't a *ponytail* forming that weird protrusion on the shadow's head. It was a hat. A hat with a single peacock feather in it!"

Ally knew that hat well. She also knew the girl who wore it well.

Or, at least, she *thought* she did. She thought they were friends. But it seemed lately Ally had been wrong about a lot of friendships.

Including this one.

"Freddie," Ally snarled, staring at the photograph on her screen. Then, with newfound determination, she shut off her phone, slipped it back into her pocket, and turned to her best friend.

"Time to go to Freddie's dorm room," she said.

It was time to question her first suspect.

Time to Investigate

*I thought Freddie was a friend.
But a good detective knows
everyone's a suspect.*

As Ally and Jane made their way to Freddie's dorm room, Ally felt a strange gnawing in her stomach at the thought of questioning Freddie Facilier. Sure, Freddie was a VK, so she was a likely suspect, but Ally had been convinced that Freddie had changed. That she'd seen the error of her villainous ways and decided to be good. And *not* steal people's stuff.

Ally and Freddie had recently bonded when they'd set out on an adventure together to the Bayou D'Orleans. At least Ally had *thought* they'd bonded. But maybe she didn't know Freddie as well as she thought she did. Maybe Freddie was still a villain through and through.

The idea unsettled her. She didn't like thinking she could be so wrong about someone. It made her doubt her own instincts, and Ally's instincts were her biggest strength. They were her secret weapon. She had to be able to rely on them if she was ever going to crack this case—or any case, for that matter.

When they arrived at Freddie's dorm room a few minutes later, Jane looked scared. Ally took a deep breath to steady her own nerves and lifted her hand to knock on the door. But before she could make contact, she heard something coming from inside. A voice.

No, not just *one* voice. *Two* voices. She looked at Jane with wide eyes.

"Who is in Freddie's room with her?" she whispered.

Perhaps Freddie had a partner in crime?

Ally was about to pound on the door and demand they fess up, but Jane grabbed her arm to stop her.

"Wait, let's listen a little longer," Jane whispered.

Ally almost protested, but then she remembered Fairy Godmother's words to her earlier: *Good detectives do rely on their instincts. But they also know when to slow down, read the clues, and think things through logically.*

Right, Ally thought. *Slow down. Read the clues. Think things through.*

If Freddie *was* in there with her accessory to the crime, then maybe listening in would provide Ally with some much-needed evidence. She lowered her hand and pressed her ear to the door instead, gesturing for Jane to do the same. The girls strained to make out the words through the thick wood.

"Why are you doing this?" a voice asked. It definitely belonged to Freddie. Ally recognized the deep, almost husky, quality of it.

"I'm just having some fun," the other voice replied, but as hard as she tried, Ally couldn't determine *whose* voice it was. It was definitely female and it seemed familiar, but Ally couldn't place it.

"You're going to get in trouble," Freddie said sternly.

"Relax, Freddie," the other voice said. "I'm disappointed in you. Auradon Prep has really turned you into such a softy. Look what else I stole."

"Stole?" Ally mouthed to Jane, nearly buzzing

with excitement. She pressed her ear harder against the door. Ally heard some kind of muffled noise, and then Freddie gasped. "That looks really valuable!"

"Exactly," the other girl replied. "Pretty wicked, huh? So easy to steal, too. The people around here are way too trusting. It's sad, really."

"You should give that back," Freddie said.

The girl sounded scandalized by the idea. "Give it *back*? Why would I do that? Geez, Freddster, you really *have* gone soft on me. There's no way I'm giving anything back. In fact, I have *big* future plans for this place."

Freddie sighed. "Must you terrorize everyone?"

The other girl giggled. "Of course! That's the pirate's life!"

Pirate's life? Ally thought curiously, and then it hit her.

Frosted tea cakes!

Ally's mind was reeling. How could she have not seen it before? How could she have not realized? It seemed so obvious! A ponytailed shadow? Someone known for stealing stuff? A villain who already knew the ins and outs of the entire school because she'd spent a week sneaking around, pulling pranks on everyone?

Ally's eyes widened in shock as she whispered the truth to her best friend. "CJ Hook is back!"

A Waiting Game

I can't concentrate on my Spirit Weekend banner. Not at a time like this.

Everyone around Ally at the party was creating these beautiful blue-and-gold masterpieces with fancy lettering and pictures of Fighting Knights, and Ally had been dragging her paintbrush around in aimless circles for the past ten minutes. She was just far too distracted by what she had discovered to focus on banners. Apparently Jane was a better actress than Ally was, because Jane was at another table, chatting with the others and painting her banner like it was just another normal day at Auradon Prep. Ally had no idea how she did it.

Ally couldn't focus. All she could think about was

CJ Hook! Back in Auradon! Hiding out in Freddie's dorm room again!

All the clues lined up. CJ matched Jane's description of the ponytailed shadow creeping outside her dorm room. *And* she had motive. CJ loved to play pranks. She had probably gobbled up that cake just to mess with the big Spirit Weekend festivities. That was definitely CJ's style. After all, she'd attempted to ruin the Neon Lights Ball, too. As for the watch, Ally was *sure* that was the valuable thing Freddie had mentioned. CJ was probably planning to sell it. Even Jane had agreed it was obvious after hearing that conversation. But then they'd had to rush to the banner-painting event.

Now Ally just had to figure out what to do with her newfound information. She suddenly remembered the promise she'd made to Fairy Godmother. She'd said that if she ever thought a crime had been committed, she'd go straight to the headmistress instead of trying to deal with it on her own. But she also knew if she went to Fairy Godmother with the information that CJ was back and wreaking havoc on the school again, then Fairy Godmother would deal with it on her own and Ally would get none of the credit for figuring it out.

And Ally was *not* about to lose this victory. She needed this. She needed to be the hero, for once, instead of the joke. She needed everyone to see that she was a real detective, who solved *real* mysteries.

She could just picture it now: Unveiling CJ to the whole school. Revealing the truth about the stolen cake and necklace. Everyone would gasp in shock. They'd pat Ally on the back, offering their congratulations and praise on a detective job well done. Then Mal would smile at her and say . . .

"Hey, Ally. What are you painting over there?"

Ally blinked and looked up at Mal, who was staring at her from across the table. "What?" Ally asked, confused.

"Sorry," Mal said, sharing a knowing look with Evie. "I didn't mean to interrupt your visit to Ally Land."

Evie tilted her head to study Ally's banner. Ally glanced down at it, too. Her mindless painting had resulted in an unsightly blue blob.

"I like it," Evie said kindly. "It looks like the profile of a prince."

Mal rolled her eyes. "Everything looks like the profile of a prince to you." But then she walked over and peered at the banner from a new angle. "Huh. Actually, you're right. It looks like Ben. See, there's his nose, his ears, and there's that little flip his hair does when he's playing tourney."

"Yeah!" Evie said excitedly.

While Evie and Mal continued to discuss the resemblance of Ally's blue blob to Mal's boyfriend, Ally tuned out again. A plan was already forming in her mind. A plan that would finally get her the glory she knew she deserved.

"I have to go," Ally announced suddenly, dropping her paintbrush into the bucket of water on the table.

"Go?" asked Evie. "Go where? Aren't you going to finish Ben's portrait?"

But Ally didn't answer. She was already darting away from the carnival grounds, a girl on a mission.

By the next morning, Ally had it all figured out. Her plan was fully formed. She barged into Jane's room without knocking and closed the door behind her. Jane was still in her pajamas, her hair unbrushed.

"Ally?" Jane asked, surprised. "I've been trying to find you since you ran off after the banner painting yesterday."

"Sorry. I had to be alone for a bit. I needed to come up with a plan. But I figured it out: how to catch CJ Hook red-handed!"

"Well, I did some thinking last night, too," Jane said slowly, "and I'm having some little doubts about accusing Freddie. It just seems really harsh. I mean, how can you know for sure—"

Ally harrumphed, cutting Jane off. "Because I just do! Detectives rely on instinct and I have that in hearts."

"I think you mean 'in spades,'" Jane said.

Ally squinted. "No, I mean I have it in hearts." She put her hand to her chest. "Instinct comes from the heart. But the point is, CJ is back, she's wreaking havoc on the school again, and I need to expose her. *We* need to expose her."

Jane looked taken aback and a bit nervous. *"We?"*

"Yes," Ally said, as though it were obvious. "I need your help exposing her."

"And how do you expect us to do that?"

Ally was prepared for the question. She had been

up all night thinking about it. She needed a plan that would guarantee maximum shock value. Something dramatic. Something with flair. And most important, something that would prove once and for all that Ally was a good detective.

"We need to gather up as many people as we can and bring them to Freddie's dorm room. Then we'll demand that Freddie open the door. She won't be able to refuse with all of those people standing there. When I reveal CJ to be hiding inside, everyone will be there to see it and then no one can deny that I was right."

Jane stared at Ally with a strange expression on her face. Ally could tell Jane wasn't exactly on board with this plan. "And why do you need *my* help for this?" Jane asked.

"I need you to back me up. I need your help rallying everyone. No one believes anything I have to say. Everyone thinks I'm just a silly girl who makes things up in her head. They won't follow me anywhere." She took a breath and gave Jane a pointed look. "But they'll follow *you*."

Jane pursed her lips, contemplating. "But why do we need to catch her at all? Why can't we just tell my mom and let her handle it? That's her job. And that's what we're supposed to do."

Ally sighed. She knew Jane would go straight to "the rules." The "right" thing to do. "Do you really want to tell your mum that you were so irresponsible with her valuable family heirloom that it was stolen?"

Jane bit her lip, clearly not having thought of that. Then she shook her head. "No, you're right. Maybe your way is better."

Ally smiled, pleased with herself. "Of course my way is better. I use Ally logic."

Jane's face scrunched in confusion. "What's Ally logic?"

Ally waved this away. "Not important. Anyway, let's discuss the plan of how we're going to get everyone to Freddie's room."

"Wait," Jane said, still looking uncertain. "Maybe we should be one hundred percent certain about this before we go through with it."

"I *am* one hundred percent certain," Ally said, losing patience.

"But we don't have any *evidence* that it was CJ who took the watch or ate the cake. Maybe we should try to gather some more clues before we just go marching in there and accusing her."

Ally crossed her arms over her chest. "Like what?"

Just then, the two girls jumped and turned toward the window of Jane's dorm room, their eyes wide with alarm.

Outside, somewhere on the Auradon Prep campus, someone was screaming.

TICKTOCK

As soon as we heard the screaming, we ran straight to the carnival grounds, hoping we weren't too late.

Audrey stood in the middle of a chaotic mess of Spirit Weekend banners, which were strewn about on the ground. Except they didn't look much like Spirit Weekend banners anymore; now they looked more like an explosion of paint on paper.

"What happened?" Ally asked immediately.

Audrey reeled on her, her eyes wide with anger. "What does it *look* like? Someone ruined the banners. All of them! I hung them out to dry last night after the party and now they're all a mess!"

Ally picked up the banner she'd seen Evie working

on before she'd left the night before. It had been completely destroyed. Ally was unable to make out any of the letters.

"Who would do this?" Audrey cried. "Who would ruin Spirit Weekend like this?"

Jane and Ally exchanged a knowing look. They both knew full well who would do something like this.

"CJ?" Jane mouthed to Ally, and Ally nodded her head decisively.

This was clearly part of CJ's big plan. She was infamous for being a prankster. She'd tried to ruin the Neon Lights Ball, and now she was trying to ruin Spirit Weekend, too! Well, not if Ally had anything to say about it.

More people were arriving at the carnival grounds by the second. It seemed everyone was following the sounds of Audrey's shrieks just as Jane and Ally had. Within a few minutes, what looked like half the student population was gathered around the paint catastrophe.

"Maybe it was a gust of wind," Lonnie suggested, picking up her own destroyed banner with the tips of her fingers, like she was afraid it might bite her.

"Don't be ridiculous," Audrey snapped. "The weather is perfect today. It's perfect every day!"

"Maybe it was Dude," Jay said, giving Carlos a rough nudge.

"Hey!" Carlos said. "Why does everyone blame my dog when something bad happens around here?"

"Will everyone just relax?" Freddie said, stepping forward to take control of the situation. "I know exactly who did this."

Ally and Jane looked at each other again. Was Freddie going to confess? Was she going to come clean about CJ hiding out in her dorm room again and wreaking havoc on the school?

Ally felt a pang of panic in her chest. As much as she wanted CJ caught and exposed, *she* was supposed to be the one to do it. If Freddie confessed now, Ally would lose her big moment in the spotlight. She'd lose her chance to prove to everyone what a good detective she was.

"You do?" Audrey said heatedly, pushing through the crowd to get to Freddie. She stood before Freddie with her hands on her hips, her narrowed eyes demanding an explanation.

"Of course," Freddie said, with a wave of her hand. "It's pretty obvious."

Audrey threw her hands in the air. "Then tell me already!"

Freddie flashed a smug grin, clearly enjoying the attention. "We see this kind of thing all the time back on the Isle of the Lost. This is definitely the work of a ghost."

Audrey was speechless for a moment, as though she'd forgotten how to form words. "A *what?*" she finally spat.

"A ghost," Freddie repeated. "They are such troublemakers, those ghosts."

A few people laughed nervously, as though Freddie had cracked a joke.

Ally peered over at Jane, who whispered, "What is she doing?"

"I don't know," Ally whispered back. "Covering for CJ?"

"That is *not* funny," Audrey said, her hands balled into fists. "Everyone knows there's no such thing as ghosts."

"I beg to differ," Freddie said. "My father—"

"In Auradon," Audrey added hastily. "There's no such thing as ghosts *in Auradon*."

"Actually," Evie chimed in, "that's not true. I was just reading a book in the library about spirits, and it said that they can pretty much go wherever they want."

"Stop!" Audrey yelled. "Stop this nonsense right now. We'll never get to the bottom of this if everyone is joking around."

But no one seemed to be listening to Audrey—especially not the VKs.

"Maybe," Mal began with a chuckle, "the ghost found out about our *Spirit* Weekend and got confused, thinking it was some kind of ghost party!"

"Is that possible?" Lonnie asked with a gasp. "Do ghosts get confused?"

"Of course they do," Freddie said. "Ghosts are not very *bright*."

"Yeah, in fact, they're pretty *dim*," Carlos added, and all five VKs—Mal, Evie, Carlos, Jay, and Freddie—broke out into hoots of laughter. No one else seemed to be in on the joke. They all just stared at the VKs, completely dumbfounded.

"Stop this," Audrey demanded sharply. "Stop this right now."

"Maybe the ghost will bring some friends to the concert tonight," Jay said, seemingly enjoying the effect this was having on poor Audrey.

"I bet they're all wearing their most fa-*boo*-lous dresses," Evie added.

"And jewels to *die* for," Freddie added with a chuckle.

"Well," Mal said thoughtfully, "you know a diamond is a *ghoul*'s best friend!"

The VKs busted up with laughter again, and Audrey looked like she was about to explode.

Ally knew this was it. This was the moment. It was now or never. They needed to put their plan into action.

"If someone doesn't fess up about this right now," Audrey shouted over the commotion, "then I'm going to—"

"I know who did it!" Ally announced, launching her hand into the air.

Gasps permeated the crowd and all eyes were suddenly on her. She cowered slightly at the attention but told herself to be brave. Be strong—just like Mal would do. Mal always seemed to face her fears head-on. Plus, this was what Ally had wanted all along: a chance to prove her worth. Now she had it.

"It's the same person who ate my cake and stole Jane's mother's watch and is now terrorizing our school. I know who the culprit is. And if you follow me, I will lead you to the person responsible!"

The group quieted down, and everyone was looking to one another, trying to figure out what to make of Ally's statement. Then small titters of doubt started to spread throughout the crowd.

"Are you still going on about that cake?" someone shouted.

"Give it up, Ally!" someone else yelled.

"My money's on the ghost!" came a third voice. Ally was pretty sure it was Chad Charming.

The crowd broke out into laughter, and suddenly Ally felt like she was back on that stage, being teased by everyone.

Just as she suspected, they didn't believe her.

She needed Jane. She needed her backup. But when she turned to her left, where Jane had been standing just a moment before, there was no one there.

Jane had abandoned her and left Ally all alone to fend for herself.

It felt like her heart was sinking to the bottom of her chest. How could Jane do that? She was supposed to be Ally's friend! She was supposed to—

"She's right!" Ally heard the voice from somewhere above her, and everyone fell silent. She glanced up to see Jane standing on a tall chair, towering over the group. "Ally knows who did this. She's a good detective and she's solved the case."

Ally felt a swell of pride and gratitude rise up inside her. Jane came through! She'd saved Ally! Just as best friends were supposed to do.

"So listen up," Jane continued, speaking louder than Ally had ever heard her talk. Jane was normally much more soft-spoken. Now her voice was big and bold, commanding attention. "Here's what we're going to do. We're going to follow Ally, find this criminal who's been terrorizing our school, and bring them to justice!"

Cheers rose up from the crowd. Fists pumped in the air. This was the reaction Ally had wanted all along. She just wanted people to believe her. To trust her. To respect her.

"Let's go!" Ally shouted, and she set off for the dorm rooms, feeling the supportive shadows of her friends and fellow students behind her the whole way.

In an Auradon Minute

With Jane on my side, I felt
superconfident. I was about to
bust this case wide open.

Ally led the crowd through the campus, up the dorm room steps, and down the hallway, stopping right in front of what everyone recognized as Freddie's dorm room. A few people in the crowd gasped and turned to glare at Freddie, who looked just as surprised by their destination.

But Ally knew she was pretending. Freddie was well aware of why they were all there.

"What are you doing?" Freddie asked, pushing her way through the throng of students crowded into the hallway. "Why are you stopped at my dorm room?"

"You know why," Ally said accusingly, sparking a series of murmurs in the group.

"Was it Freddie?" Ally heard someone ask.

"But I thought Freddie was good now," someone else said.

"It's like I've always said, you can't trust a VK," another person murmured.

Freddie crossed her arms over her chest. "Actually, I *don't* know why, Ally. I thought we were friends. Now you're accusing me of stealing stuff?"

"No," Ally said, setting off another round of titters. "I'm accusing you of lying to us about who did."

Freddie squinted in confusion. "What are you talking about?"

"You lied to me! To all of us! You have been harboring a criminal!"

"What?" Freddie cried.

Ally had to admit Freddie really *did* look genuinely surprised by the accusation, which made Ally's stomach do a little flip in a momentary lapse of confidence. Could it be possible she was wrong about this?

No, she told herself. *I'm right. CJ is in there. I heard her.*

Ally stood up straighter and took a deep breath.

"CJ Hook is back!" she announced to the crowd. "She stole my cake! And Jane's mother's watch! And ruined the Spirit Weekend banners." Ally turned back to Freddie and pointed at her. "And *Freddie* has been hiding her in her dorm room!"

A collective gasp rose from the group.

Ally expected Freddie to confess. To bow her head in shame and admit to the allegations. But she didn't. She just rolled her eyes and sighed. "Ally! This is ridiculous. CJ is not here."

"Well, then open your door and let us take a look for ourselves," Ally countered.

Freddie chuckled, like she knew a secret. "Fine," she said, much too casually for Ally's liking. Freddie took out the key to her dorm room, slid it into the lock, and turned. She opened the door and several students pushed their way inside behind Ally, all eager to be the first to spot the infamous CJ Hook.

But the room was empty.

"Where is she?" someone asked.

"Maybe she's hiding!" someone else said.

"Yes!" Ally cried out. "She's hiding. Search the room!"

Freddie snorted with what looked like amusement

as several students began to search under the bed and in the wardrobe and behind the curtains. But with each passing second, Ally was growing more and more anxious.

Where was CJ? Had she climbed out the window? *Did she already leave?*

"Ally," a gentle voice said, and Ally felt a hand on her shoulder. She turned to see it was Evie. "I don't think CJ is here."

"Of course she's here!" Ally snapped. "I heard Freddie talking to her yesterday! She was talking about how she had big plans to terrorize Auradon Prep *and* that she had stolen something valuable!"

Freddie began to cackle with laughter. "Is that what this is about?" she asked, her annoyance replaced with amusement. Freddie walked over to her desk and pulled out a tablet. "Yes, I talked to her yesterday," Freddie went on, swiping her fingertip across the tablet screen and then turning it around to show the group. "On *video chat*."

Video chat?

Ally took a step toward Freddie, dread blooming in her stomach as she looked at the tablet. A moment later, CJ's face filled the entire screen.

"Ahoy, mateys!" CJ's voice came crystal clear through the tablet's speakers. "Having a party without me? I'm offended." Then she hooted with laughter. "Actually, no, I'm not. Auradon Prep is such a bore compared to the excitement of Camelot Heights."

Camelot Heights?

"I mean, just look at this adorable little town. Overflowing with places to loot." CJ turned the camera away from her face and panned it around, zooming in on a nearby building. The sign on the front read:

CAMELOT HEIGHTS JEWELERS

Ally's chest squeezed with panic. CJ was in Camelot Heights? But that was on the other side of the kingdom, more than a day's journey from Auradon—which meant there was no way CJ could have been there to ruin the signs the previous night.

The dorm room was silent, but Ally's mind was reeling. She immediately replayed the conversation she'd overheard the day before.

"You're going to get in trouble."
"Relax, Freddie. I'm disappointed in you. Auradon

Prep has really turned you into such a softy. Look what else I stole."

"That looks really valuable!"

"Exactly. Pretty wicked, huh? So easy to steal, too. The people around here are way too trusting."

It had definitely been CJ's voice, but had she ever actually *said* she was in Auradon?

No. She hadn't.

"Well, I'd love to stay and chat," CJ said, "but pirate duty calls!" CJ's finger extended toward the camera, and a moment later, the screen went dark.

Ally felt her breathing grow shallow. She couldn't be wrong about this. Not again. Not in front of everyone!

"So the valuable thing she stole . . ." Ally began.

"It was a necklace," Freddie explained. "From some poor old lady. And I convinced her to return it."

"Not Fairy Godmother's watch?" Ally asked, needing confirmation.

"No," Freddie said.

Ally tapped her forehead, trying to focus her scrambled thoughts.

Freddie set the tablet down on the desk and scowled at Ally. "I can't believe, after everything we've been through together, you would think I'd do something like this."

"And I can't believe that you would yet again accuse the wrong person," Mal said, stepping up to stand next to Freddie.

"And *I* can't believe I let you drag me into this!" Jane cried.

Ally suddenly felt very small, like she'd drunk one of those Wonderland shrinking potions and was now the size of a leaf.

Her stomach clenched. She hadn't solved the crime. She'd failed. Again. She'd let her obsession with solving the mystery and satisfying her curiosity cloud her judgment—just as her mother once had long before, when she'd followed a white rabbit in a waistcoat down a rabbit hole.

Ally took a sheepish step toward the door. "Whoopsie!" she said brightly, trying to lighten the mood. "My mistake!"

But it didn't work. The energy in the air was heavy and angry. Ally could feel it pressing down on her shoulders. "Did you know," she said, forcing lightness into her voice, "that 'mistake' is actually an anagram for 'a kismet'? Which means 'meant to be'! Isn't that curious?"

No one said anything, and Ally felt like the silence was drowning her. So she kept talking. "Although, another anagram for 'mistake' is 'meat ski,' which is kind of funny, because, honestly, what's a meat ski, right? Is it a piece of meat that skis?" She was hoping for a laugh. A smile. Anything. But all she saw were stony, disappointed faces staring back at her. And the face that looked the most disappointed of them all belonged to Jane.

Whoopsie, indeed, Ally thought.

This was by far the worst "meat ski" she'd ever made.

Second Chances, Anyone?

I could feel the animosity rising off everyone like steam. It was more uncomfortable than a tea party without finger sandwiches.

"Please, let me explain," Ally said to the small group that remained in Freddie's room. After it was revealed that CJ wasn't there, most of the students had wandered down to the banquet hall, muttering something about breakfast, except for Audrey, who was ranting about going to back to the carnival grounds to try to salvage what was left of the signs. The only people left in the room with Ally were Freddie, Jane, Mal, and Evie.

"After my cake was eaten and Jane's watch went

missing," Ally tried to explain, "I thought it was connected. I thought—"

"There's no connection," Mal said with a frustrated sigh. "You have to stop trying to turn everything into some giant conspiracy. Cakes get eaten, watches get misplaced, signs get ruined; it doesn't mean there's some great criminal at work."

"Actually," Evie cut in, pursing her lips, "now that you list everything out like that, it does seem kind of *strange* that all of this would happen around the same time, doesn't it?"

Ally's hopes lifted for a moment. Was Evie taking her side? Was someone actually standing up for her? But then her hopes came crashing back down when Mal said hastily, "No. It's just a coincidence. There's no cake-eating, watch-stealing, sign-ruining bandit running amok in Auradon. Someone ate the cake and didn't want to fess up to it. Dude probably *did* destroy those signs. And Jane just forgot where she put her watch."

Ally glanced uneasily over at Jane, who up until then hadn't said a word. She'd just been silently fuming in the corner of Freddie's dorm room.

"Isn't that right, Jane?" Mal prompted.

Jane nodded. "I must have misplaced it," she said in a near whisper. But even through her soft voice, Ally could tell she was furious.

"See?" Mal said, throwing up her arms. "So, no more playing detective. No more accusing people. No more mysteries! Okay?"

Tears welled up in Ally's eyes but she hastily blinked them away. She didn't want Mal to see her cry. "Okay," she whispered.

Mal huffed. "Good. Now let's go to breakfast. I'm starving."

Everyone shuffled out of Freddie's room. Mal, Evie, and Freddie immediately disappeared down the hallway toward the banquet hall, and Ally was left alone with Jane, who wouldn't even meet Ally's eyes.

She knew she should say something to Jane. But what? Her mother always told her that you should apologize when you did something wrong. And Ally knew she had definitely done something wrong. So she sucked in a breath and said, "I'm—"

But the rest of the words never came out, because suddenly Jane was crying.

"I can't believe you did that to me, Ally!" she said through her tears. "I can't believe you dragged me into one of your silly accusations! I trusted you. I trusted that you knew what you were talking about. And now everyone thinks I'm just as bad as you are."

"Jane," Ally tried to say, but Jane didn't even let her finish. She turned on her heels and stalked down the hallway without even a glance back in Ally's direction.

Ally slumped and started toward her dorm room but changed her mind halfway there. Instead, she turned and ran out of the dorms. She darted down the paved walkway, past the lockers, and then across the tourney field, where Mal's beautiful stage and decorations were set up and ready for the concert that afternoon. Ally doubted she would be going to that. No one wanted to see *her* face around there. She didn't stop running until she was at the tea shop, the one place where she felt safe. The door jingled when she opened it, waking Dino, who was napping on a couch. He jumped down and came to slink around Ally's ankles.

Ally scooped the kitty in her arms and collapsed into a large upholstered armchair.

"I don't know what I was thinking, Dino," Ally said.

"Meow?" Dino asked with concern.

"No," Ally answered Dino's question. "It didn't go well at all. It turns out I'm not a detective. I'm not a sleuth. I tried to find patterns where they didn't even exist. I tried to apply Ally logic and it only made things worse."

Dino looked confused. "Meow?"

"It means logic with a twist. But it doesn't matter, because Ally logic failed. *I* failed. I failed everyone—Jane, Mal, Evie, Freddie, Audrey. But mostly, I failed myself."

Dino tried his best to console her by curling up next to her.

Ally let out a sad laugh. "You're right, kitty. I didn't fail *you*. Thank you for that."

But even that small reassurance from her friend couldn't stop the tears from falling. Ally held the cat close to her and buried her face in his soft fur. Normally Dino didn't like being held so tightly. Normally he squirmed and tried to get loose. But this time, he seemed to understand how much Ally needed him, because he just sat there, purring, letting Ally's giant tears soak his fur.

EVEN A BROKEN CLOCK IS RIGHT TWICE A DAY

Unfortunately, I was wrong twice
in less than twenty-four hours.
And it seemed that everyone
hated me, even my best friend.

Ally fell asleep in the tea shop with Dino cradled in her arms. As she slept, she dreamt. Unlike her mother, Ally didn't dream of white rabbits and talking caterpillars and red queens. Instead, Ally dreamt of her friends. Jane and Mal and Evie and Freddie and Audrey. She could see all of their disappointed faces spinning around her, like they were on a high-speed carousel and she was stuck in the center.

Jane, whom she'd dragged into this nonsense.

Mal, who had gotten so frustrated with her.

Evie, who had always tried to make her feel better.

Freddie, who she had falsely accused of harboring a criminal.

And Audrey, who was out there right now, trying to fix what was left of her Spirit Weekend banners.

Ally jolted awake and looked at the clock on the wall of the tea shop. She'd only been asleep for thirty minutes, but it was long enough for her to come to a conclusion.

Her mother always told her that if you hurt someone's feelings, you should apologize. If you break something, you should try to fix it. Ally knew she couldn't undo what she'd done. She couldn't un-ask for Jane's help or un-accuse Freddie of hiding CJ in her room.

But there was one place where she *could* help.

So Ally stood up, said good-bye to Dino, and headed back toward the carnival grounds. When she arrived, she found the grounds empty, apart from the ruined banners. Audrey had evidently given up trying to fix them. And Ally couldn't blame her. They didn't look fixable. All the writing had been smeared and all the carefully painted pictures had turned into illogical messes.

Who could have done this? Ally thought. But she quickly stopped herself before her thoughts went too far down that road.

Stop trying to solve everything. Stop trying to find a pattern. Just help clean up.

So that's exactly what Ally did. She started picking up the ruined banners and depositing them in the Dumpster. Everyone's hard work, in the trash.

When she picked up her own banner—the amorphous blue glob—she remembered how Evie and Mal had thought it looked like Ben. Ally blinked and stared down at her paper, trying to see what Evie and Mal had seen. She squinted at the nondescript glob of blue paint, turning the paper in a circle, trying to study it from every angle. But no matter how hard she stared at it, she just couldn't see what her friends had seen.

Ally had always viewed things differently, even as a child. Her mother told her it was her hidden strength, but now it just seemed like her weakness. She wished she could see things like everyone else. She wished she could see a mural on a wall as just a mural on a wall. Or an eaten cake and lost watch and ruined signs as nothing more than random occurrences. She wished she could see a prince in this blob, but she just couldn't.

All she saw was a blob.

With a sigh, Ally walked over to the Dumpster and lifted the lid. But just before she stuffed the banner inside, something peculiar caught her eye.

Wait a minute. . . .

Ally squinted at the banner, her vision zeroing in on the bottom left corner of the sign.

What is that?

What had originally looked like just a random splattering of paint—a mishap from whatever banner-ruining escapade had happened there—upon closer inspection, seemed to have a shape.

Are those . . . ?

Ally shook her head. No. They couldn't be.

But the closer she looked, the more certain she became.

Those were footprints. Tiny footprints. Like those belonging to a small animal of some kind.

Dude? Ally immediately guessed. Was Mal right? Had Dude run through there and demolished all the paintings?

But for some reason, Ally wasn't convinced. These didn't look like dog prints. Not at all.

What kind of creature left prints this shape? Ally quickly pulled out her phone and did a search. As she waited for the results, she felt bread-and-butterflies fluttering in her stomach. What kind of animal could she be dealing with? A bear, perhaps? Or a cougar?

Ally was not afraid of cougars. She had met one once in the swamp in the Bayou D'Orleans when she'd gone there with Freddie and Jordan on an epic adventure. But that was a whole other story.

The results appeared on her screen, and Ally let out a loud gasp as the banner slipped from her hands and floated to the ground.

What?

It couldn't be . . . could it?

Ally could feel pieces falling into place in her mind. She could feel the familiar sensation of details rearranging themselves into a pattern, like letters of an anagram mixing up to spell a new word with a new meaning.

A gobbled-up carrot cake.

A stolen watch.

Ruined signs.

Everyone said they weren't connected. But Ally knew in her heart of hearts that wasn't true. They *were* connected. By the very thing that left behind these footprints.

Ally let out a giddy yip, scooped up the fallen banner, and took off at a run. She didn't stop until she was banging on Jane's dorm room door. Jane opened it and her eyes immediately narrowed. "What are you doing here?" she asked crossly.

"I know who did it!" Ally announced proudly, her face lit up like a firework. "Jane, I solved the mystery!"

TODAY IS A GIFT

That's why they call it the present,
right? I had figured out who was behind
all the curious things happening in
Auradon. And I had to tell Jane.

"I don't want anything to do with this." Jane immediately started to close the door on Ally, but Ally stopped it with her foot and pushed her way inside.

"Just listen," Ally urged. "Remember when the VKs were joking about a ghost ruining the signs?"

Jane crossed her arms over her chest. "Ally, I'm still mad at you. And I don't want to talk to you, especially about *this*."

Ally continued. "Well, it turned out they weren't that far off about the ghost."

Jane took the bait. "Wait. What are you talking about?"

"The culprit! The thief responsible for everything that's happened around here. It isn't *human*."

Jane looked extremely skeptical, like she didn't even want to reply. But Ally could tell Jane's curiosity was winning. They were best friends, after all. If anyone knew how to get Jane's attention, it was Ally.

"Okay, if it's not human, what is it?" Jane finally asked.

Ally inhaled deeply. She knew that what she was about to say would seem odd to someone as logical as Jane, but she had to at least *try* to make her understand. Ally pushed the banner into Jane's hands. She pointed at the small footprints in the corner. "Look at that. Look at those prints."

Jane shrugged. "Dude?"

"No. Those aren't dog prints."

"Then what are they?"

Ally exhaled slowly and then announced, "They're *rabbit* prints."

Jane squinted at her for a long time, probably trying to decide if Ally was for real or not. "Rabbit prints," Jane repeated dubiously. "Are you seriously trying to tell me that a rabbit stole my mother's watch?"

"Not just any rabbit," Ally explained eagerly. "The kind of rabbit who talks and wears waistcoats and is obsessed with *watches*." She expected Jane to shout out the answer right away, but when she didn't, Ally sighed and said, "The *White* Rabbit!"

Jane looked at Ally like she was crazy. "Like from Wonderland?"

Ally nodded. "Except he's not in Wonderland anymore. Somehow, he's here. In Auradon. Eating *carrot* cakes, and destroying Spirit Weekend banners, and stealing watches. Get it? Watches! He's obsessed with time! All the clues add up. The thing on the head of the shadow you saw? It wasn't a ponytail, it was a set of rabbit ears! And the pattering of feet you heard in the hallway? Those were *his* feet."

Jane sighed, clearly growing impatient with her. "Ally, I really don't want to get involved."

"I know you think I'm crazy," Ally said, "but I assure you, it all makes sense. Look at this." Ally reached into the pocket of her dress, and a moment later, she pulled out a long gold chain. On the end of it dangled the old, broken pocket watch.

"Mum's pocket watch!" Ally cried. "I'd completely forgotten about it. Until I remembered it, of course!"

"Of course," Jane said sarcastically.

"And I remembered that when I broke it, the clock stopped. At one thirty p.m.! It was the connection I'd been looking for!" Ally continued.

Jane obviously wasn't following. And she looked like she was about to kick Ally right out of her dorm room. Ally knew she had to talk fast if she was going to convince Jane her theory was right.

"This pocket watch is some kind of clue. You see, it's my mum's. From Wonderland. She said it was very old and very fragile, and she once warned me that I should never ever break it. But then yesterday, I broke it. Well, technically Dino broke it, but that's not important. What *is* important is that it's dead. Its heart stopped."

"Watches don't have hearts," Jane pointed out grumpily.

"They most certainly do!" Ally said defensively. "How else would I be able to tell that the watch is dead? It stopped at exactly one thirty p.m., just minutes before the cake was eaten. Then shortly after that, your watch disappeared. Don't you understand?"

Jane massaged her forehead, like this whole thing was giving her a headache. "No, I don't. I don't understand anything."

Ally pointed at the large crack on the glass face of the watch. "I think breaking this watch is somehow connected to the White Rabbit coming here to Auradon. Everything that has gone wrong around here started when this watch broke, which means . . ."

Ally's voice trailed off as a troubling feeling settled over her. Her shoulders slouched. Her face fell. The room seemed to darken.

"Wait. It means this is all my fault," she finally whispered, almost too quietly for anyone else to hear. "All this time I've been looking for the person responsible, when actually *I've* been the person responsible."

Ally was genuinely distressed. She felt like she might burst into tears.

At this, Jane seemed to soften a little bit, as though her anger about everything that had happened couldn't compete with the empathy she felt for her friend.

"Well, I'm sure that's not true," Jane said consolingly. "You just said that Dino broke the watch, not you."

"Yes, but I found it. And instead of giving it straight to my mum, I decided I wanted to keep it and clean it up. That's how it got broken. If Audrey finds out that it's *my* fault the signs were ruined, then she'll convince everyone to hate me!" Ally felt tears welling up as she stared pleadingly into the eyes of her best friend.

Jane stared back, her own eyes conflicted. And then Ally saw the shift in Jane's expression. Her earlier resolve to not get involved in any more madness was quickly being replaced by a look of protectiveness as years' worth of friendship shone through the rain cloud that had settled over the girls.

"Well," Jane said meekly, fidgeting with the hem of her dress, "we won't tell Audrey. We won't tell anyone. Until we figure this out."

Ally exhaled and sniffled, feeling relieved to hear Jane say that. It wasn't total forgiveness, but at least she knew her secret was safe.

Jane took the watch from Ally and ran her hand

over the cracked glass. Ally had to admit Jane looked slightly intrigued by the broken heirloom.

"So, let's say this backward logic of yours makes sense," Jane began hesitantly.

"It *does* make sense," Ally affirmed.

"Fine," Jane agreed. "If all of this is true, then *why* would the White Rabbit do all of these things? Like, why would he snatch your cake and steal my watch and ruin all of the Spirit Weekend signs? He's not a villain, right?"

Ally pursed her lips in thought. "No, not really. He's . . . well, he's complicated. I mean, he didn't get banished to the Isle of the Lost like all the other villains, but he was loyal to the Queen of Hearts, who *was* a villain. But mostly because he was just terrified of losing his head, like everyone else. So I don't think he's evil, per se. According to Mum, he was always just very anxious and restless." Ally stopped and studied Jane's expression for a moment, trying to determine what her friend was thinking.

"You do believe me, right?" Ally asked.

Jane didn't say anything for a long time. Then she murmured, "I don't know, Ally. This all just seems a little . . ."

"Mad, I know," Ally said with a sigh. "And I understand if you don't want to get involved again. Especially after what happened last time. But I also know that if I don't figure out how he got here or how to stop him from wreaking havoc on our school, then he'll do something much worse. Like ruin Mal's concert."

"That would be bad," Jane agreed. "Mal's been planning this surprise for Ben for months. So what are you going to do? Try to catch him?"

Ally immediately shook her head. "Mum tried that once. It got her into a whole lot of trouble. If there's one thing I learned growing up, it's that you don't go chasing white rabbits."

"Then what?"

Ally tapped her forehead, trying to organize her thoughts. Meanwhile, Jane turned the watch around and around in her palm, thinking.

And that's when Ally saw it.

The engraving on the back!

"Wait!" she said, reaching out to take the pocket watch back from Jane. She turned it over to study the letters etched into the metal surface. Ally had first seen the words when she found the watch under the floorboard.

"I bet *he* could help!"

Jane leaned in and read the engraving.

" 'Mr. Weiden'?" Jane asked. "Who's that?"

"The watchmaker! It has to be. Watchmakers always stamp their names into the backs of the watches they make. And if he made this watch, then he might know how it's connected to the White Rabbit."

Ally immediately pulled out her phone and opened a search. She typed in MR. WEIDEN WATCHMAKER. Both girls stared at the phone in anticipation.

When the results came back, Ally felt her stomach clench with disappointment.

"It says there is no result for 'Mr. Weiden watchmaker,' " Jane said.

Ally harrumphed. "Hmmm. He must not be listed."

"Maybe you should ask your mom about this," Jane suggested.

Ally shook her head. "I don't want to ask Mum. For starters, I'd have to admit that I broke the watch and she'll undoubtedly be cross about that. Plus, she always acts a little peculiar when I ask her questions about Wonderland. Like she doesn't want to think about it. She won't even visit Tweedleton because . . ."

Ally's voice trailed off again and she was suddenly lost in her own thoughts.

"Ally?" Jane asked, waving a hand in front of her face. "Hello!"

Jane's voice sounded like it was coming from the end of a long tunnel.

Ally blinked and focused back on her friend.

"I have to go there!" Ally announced decidedly.

Jane squinted, clearly not able to keep up. "Go where?"

"To Tweedleton! It's where a bunch of Mum's Wonderland friends retired. There has to be someone there who knows about this watch, someone who can help me understand what happened and how to fix it so I can save Spirit Weekend!"

"How are you going to get there?" Jane asked apprehensively. "You're not old enough to drive and I don't think anyone here is in the mood to give you a ride right now."

"Hmmm," Ally said, pretending to think very hard. "If only I knew someone who could magically turn regular items into modes of transportation.

Someone whose mother, perhaps, is famous for doing just that." She stared pointedly at Jane until Jane understood.

"No," Jane replied immediately. "Last time I helped you out, I ended up completely humiliating myself. Plus, I'm not allowed to use my magic."

"Oh, c'mon," Ally begged. "If you won't do it for me, do it for the White Rabbit. Do it for Spirit Weekend!" Ally tilted her head and stared at Jane with large pleading blue eyes.

Jane looked like she was having some kind of argument inside her own head. Finally, she said, "Fine. I'll do it. To get my mom's watch back." Jane paused for a moment, before quickly adding, "And to save Spirit Weekend."

The Clock Is Ticking

I didn't want to be late for our very important date . . . in Tweedleton!

The two girls stood in the center of the tea shop, searching for something for Jane to transform.

"A teacup?" Ally suggested, wondering what kind of vehicle a teacup would turn into.

Jane shook her head. "I'd feel more comfortable with food. My mom always preferred vegetables."

Ally ran into the kitchen and returned a moment later holding a bright-green ripe cucumber. "How about this? It was the only produce I could find. We use them for cucumber sandwiches."

Jane took it and turned it around in her hand, examining it from all angles. "This could work."

"Great!" Ally exclaimed.

But Jane didn't move. She just continued to stare at the cucumber with hesitation.

"What?" Ally asked. "Wrong vegetable? Wrong color? Wrong shape? I think I could probably find some old cabbage in the Dumpster out back."

"No," Jane said, biting her lip. "I just . . . you really think that someone in Tweedleton will be able to tell you how the White Rabbit got into Auradon?"

"Of course," Ally said with certainty. "The White Rabbit lives in Wonderland and these people in Tweedleton are all originally *from* Wonderland, so they have to be able to help."

Jane nodded. "I guess that sounds logical."

There was that word again. Ally really disliked that word. "What's so great about being logical anyway?" Ally asked.

"Because it means that something makes sense and follows order and rules."

Ally crinkled her nose. "That sounds like a horrible thing to be. I don't follow any order or any rules."

"I hadn't noticed," Jane said sarcastically.

"And you know?" Ally went on, ignoring Jane's

jab. "You could probably stand to be a little un-logical every once in a while, as well."

"It's *il*logical," Jane corrected. "Not *un*-logical."

Ally frowned. "That makes no sense at all!"

Jane giggled. It was the first time Ally had heard her laugh in a long time. It was a nice sound, and it made Ally giggle, too. "I guess maybe that's the point."

"Well, I say it's *un*-logical," Ally maintained. "And that's exactly what I strive to be. Un-logical."

Jane laughed again. "Then congratulations, Ally. Because you are the most *un*-logical person I know."

Ally beamed. "Thank you." Then her smile fell for a moment. "Wait, is that a compliment?"

Jane nodded. "Absolutely. Now let's do this." She turned and carried the cucumber out the door.

Ally clapped her hands and followed. "Goody! I just love magic. What do you think you'll be able to turn the cucumber into? A glamorous trolley? A first-class airplane? A stretch limo?"

Jane set the cucumber down on the ground, took a step back, and called out, "Bibbidi-Bobbidi-Boo!"

An explosion of green sparkles and smoke erupted

around the cucumber, and a second later, Jane and Ally were staring at a huge . . .

Ally tilted her head. "Uh, what is that, exactly?"

Jane studied it, too, trying to make sense of what she had conjured. "I think it's a canoe."

It was indeed a canoe. A long green canoe with two seats and paddles attached to the sides.

Ally didn't want to be rude. After all, Jane was using her magic to help her out, and it seemed the two of them were maybe starting to get along again. But there was no way she was going to get to Tweedleton in a *canoe*. "Um, Jane, *darling*," she said as politely as she could. "This is lovely. Simply *lovely*. But the problem is, Tweedleton is a landlocked town. I can't very well travel there by water."

Jane winced. "Oh. Whoops. My bad. I'm still getting the hang of this whole magic thing. I haven't gotten it completely under control yet. I still don't know what will come out when I say the words 'Bibbidi-Bobbidi-Boo.' "

Suddenly, there was another blast of green glitter. It surprised the girls, who both jumped back from the transforming canoe. After the puffs of smoke had cleared, Ally stared at the new vehicle in front of them and her hopes came crashing to the ground. Maybe asking Jane for help wasn't the best idea she'd ever had.

"And that's a bicycle," Ally said blankly.

"A bicycle built for two," Jane corrected, as if that made all the difference.

And it *was* different, all right. Ally had never seen a bicycle for two people before. It looked like someone had taken two normal bicycles and glued them together, creating one long bike with two seats, two sets of pedals, and one handlebar in the front.

Once again, Ally didn't want to seem ungrateful, but she was feeling a little bit hopeless at the moment. "It's *divine*, really," she said, stepping forward to give the bike a tap. "And so sturdy. Well, done, you. I'm just not sure how I'm supposed to get to Tweedleton on this. Perhaps you can whip me up something else?"

Jane shook her head solemnly. "I don't think it's such a good idea to transform it again. You might risk losing quality. I think this is the best I'm going to be able to do."

Ally bit her lip, trying to think of a way to turn this dead end around. "Right, then," she said brightly.

"No problem. I'm sure this is perfectly simple to ride once I get the hang of it."

Ally hiked up her blue-and-white dress and stepped over the bike, sitting down on the first seat. She positioned her feet on the pedals, took a deep breath, and pushed off, pumping her legs. She was able to maneuver the bike about three feet forward, but it was simply too big for just one person and she eventually toppled over onto the grass.

"Oof!" she cried out.

Jane cringed. "Ally, I—"

"Not to worry!" Ally called, hopping back up and attempting to mount the bike again. "I just need a little more practice. I'm sure it's just like riding a bike."

"Ally," Jane said more sternly. "Stop. Just stop."

Ally brought her feet to the ground and fought to steady the long bike, which wobbled beneath her. "What?"

Jane looked like she was trying hard not to laugh. "First of all, you need a helmet. And second of all, I'm coming with you."

Ally felt a lump of gratitude form in her throat. "You're going to come with me?"

"Well, someone needs to help you ride that bike."

"But I thought you were cross with me," Ally said. "For making you look like a fool in front of everyone."

Jane stared at her feet. "I am. I mean, I *was*."

Ally immediately lightened at Jane's use of the past tense, and she let out a huge sigh of relief. "So does this mean you finally believe me?"

Jane thought about that for such a long time, Ally began to fidget. Then Jane spoke very softly. "I guess it doesn't matter if I believe you. I believe *in* you."

Ally felt her whole body warm with appreciation toward her best friend. "Thank you, Jane. For not running off and telling everyone this is all my fault."

"I don't think it *is* all your fault."

"Yes, well, thank you for keeping my secret."

Jane shrugged. "That's what friends do."

Ally felt a pang at the word *friends*. She certainly hadn't been a very good one to Jane lately. She'd been so obsessed with proving to everyone she could solve a mystery that she hadn't stopped to think how her obsession would affect Jane. "And I'm sorry," Ally added quickly. "For . . . everything."

"It's okay," Jane said. "I . . . I know you were just trying to help me get my mom's watch back. And

I can't really blame you for that. Even though your methods might be a little illogical"—Ally shot her a look—"sorry, *un*-logical," Jane corrected, "I know your heart is in the right place."

Ally put her hand to her chest, feeling her heartbeat. "Well, I should hope so. If it were in my foot, I'm afraid I'd be dead."

Jane giggled. "You always find the most peculiar ways to see things. I really love that about you."

Ally grinned. "And I love how loyal of a friend you are." The two girls stood there, smiling at each other, before Ally realized they were losing time. "C'mon. We're late! For a very important date!"

Jane looked confused. "Did you call someone in Tweedleton and make an appointment?"

Ally shook her head. "No, silly. It's just an expression."

Jane ran over and was about to hop on the bike, but something made her pause. She glanced around, and after spotting two mushrooms growing in the grass nearby, cried out, "Bibbidi-Bobbidi-Boo!" The mushrooms instantly grew and morphed into two light brown bike helmets. Jane picked them up, handed one to Ally, and placed the other atop her own head.

"Not bad," Ally said, fastening the strap on hers. "Although they do smell a little like fungus."

Jane giggled and hopped on the back seat of the bike. Ally was just about to push off and start pedaling toward Tweedleton when a thought came to her. She turned around to face Jane. "Wait a minute. Should we ask your mum if we can go? It's against the rules to leave campus without permission."

Jane shrugged. "If I've learned anything from you, Ally, it's that sometimes rules need to bend."

Slowly but Surely

Normally, Tweedleton is about an hour
bike ride from Auradon Prep. But nothing
I do is really normal, now is it?

One would think that with two people pedaling it would take only half that time, but with Jane and Ally, it took almost twice as long. Mostly because they kept stopping along the way to argue about who was pedaling more and who should sit in the front seat to steer.

At first Ally was in the front, so she couldn't see Jane behind her. Going up a particularly steep hill, Ally called back, "Are you even pedaling at all?" Except the words came out more like wheezes, because Ally was working so hard she was out of breath.

"Yes!" Jane tried to shout, but that also came out

like a wheeze. "I'm . . . pedaling . . . as . . . hard . . . as . . . I . . . can!"

"Well, it must not be very hard," Ally complained, putting her foot down to stop the bike. "Because it feels like I'm doing all the work up here."

Jane fought to catch her breath. "No, I'm doing all the work back *here*. You're just sitting up there and steering."

Ally put her hands on her hips and turned around to face Jane. "There's no *way* you're doing all the work."

"Going uphill on a tandem bike automatically puts the brunt of the work on the backseat."

Ally scoffed at that. "Is this another one of your logical things?"

"Actually, it's a physics thing," Jane corrected.

"Well, I don't care if it's a biochemistronomy thing! I am definitely pedaling harder than you."

"Biochemistronomy is not a thing," Jane argued.

"It sure is," Ally countered. "It even has some exquisite anagrams like . . ." She tapped her forehead. " 'Misty moon brioche,' and 'shiny robotic memo,' and 'bionic theory moms.' Ooh! That would make a marvelous name for a punk rock band, don't you agree?"

"Ally! Focus!" Jane snapped her fingers in front of Ally's face. "We have less than five hours before the concert starts. If you want to fix that watch and keep the White Rabbit from ruining Mal's big concert surprise, we need to keep going."

"Fine," Ally huffed. "But I'm getting in the back."

"Fine by me."

The two girls swapped places and Ally soon realized that Jane might have been right. Not only was the backseat harder, it was also frustrating because she couldn't see around Jane and there was no way to control the bike. Jane was doing all the steering and she was doing a dreadful job at it.

"Veer left!" Ally shouted when they were coasting down another hill, heading straight toward a patch of trees on the side of the road.

"I've got it!" Jane shouted back.

"No, you don't got it! We're going to crash!"

They didn't crash. But they came close. So close that Ally insisted on being in the front again. And so it went for the rest of the way to Tweedleton.

Ally had heard stories about the town of Tweedleton from her mother, and she'd always wanted to go there. She'd seen pictures of it before and located it on maps, but nothing could have quite prepared her for seeing it in person.

The town's entrance was marked by a high steel archway with the word TWEEDLETON carved out of the metal. They set the bike aside and decided to continue into town on foot. Stepping under that archway and onto the stone path felt like stepping right through the rabbit hole to Wonderland. All around them were thick green forest, tall colorful flowers, shrubs that made Ally feel the size of an ant, and handwritten wooden signs pointing in every direction.

Once they reached the center of the town—which required a dizzying walk through a maze of high groomed hedges—Ally marveled at all the various statues in the shapes of caterpillars, playing cards, and Cheshire cats. And the little shops had the most peculiar names, like Dormouse and Sons' Mattress Company, Spades' Garden Supplies, Ravens and Writing Desks, and The Walrus's Oyster Shack (except *Walrus* had been crossed out and the word *Carpenter* had been written in, as if the restaurant had recently changed ownership).

Ally smiled, taking it all in. Just being there made Ally feel connected to her mother, and that made her quite happy.

"This place is really weird," Jane said, spinning in a slow circle.

"It's not weird," Ally corrected. "It's curious. There's a difference."

"Well, who are we supposed to talk to?" Jane asked. The town appeared to be deserted. The main square was completely empty, as though someone had just evacuated the streets.

"Maybe we should try one of the shops?"

Ally walked up to the Ravens and Writing Desks store and peered through the window. The shop was also empty apart from the unusual merchandise lining the shelves. One half of the shop was filled with nothing but small black ravens sitting in bird cages, while the other half of the shop was stocked with nothing but writing desks.

"What a peculiar combination," Ally mused, stepping away from the glass.

"Anyone in there?" Jane asked.

Ally shook her head. "Not a single one."

"That's odd," Jane said. "I wonder where every-one is."

"At the party, naturally," came a voice. Actually, it sounded more like *two* voices saying the exact same thing at the exact same time.

Jane and Ally spun around, searching for the source of the sound.

"Who said that?" Ally asked.

"We did," the curious double voice said. "Obviously."

Ally and Jane shared a dubious look. They still couldn't see where the voices were coming from.

"Who are you?" Ally asked, hoping to lure out their mysterious new friends.

But still no one appeared. Ally heard a quiet *tsk, tsk, tsk* sound, and then one of the voices whispered, "She doesn't know who we are."

"Everyone knows who we are," the other voice replied.

"She must be from out of town," the first voice reasoned.

"Precisely," the second voice agreed.

"We *are* from out of town," Jane called in no

particular direction, since neither of the girls knew where the voices were coming from.

"But we want to know more about your town," Ally put in. "And perhaps ask you some questions."

"Questions?" the voices said eagerly, back in perfect sync with each other. "We love questions. And songs!"

"Us too," Jane said uneasily.

"Have a seat, then," the voices commanded. "Comfortably."

Ally and Jane both glanced around before finally spotting a small park bench behind them. The girls shared another look before shrugging and taking a seat on the bench.

They waited. The problem was they had no idea what they were waiting for, or how long it would take.

Then, suddenly, two small boys crawled out from beneath the bench, startling Ally and Jane. The boys were dressed in matching uniforms of red shorts with blue belts, yellow polo shirts, and red caps on their heads. They looked perfectly identical, from their clothes to their little button noses to the way they stood side by side before Ally and Jane, hands on their hips, feet slightly turned out. Ally felt her eyes cross. It was as though she were looking at mirror reflections of the same person.

"Oh! You're twins!" Ally said, pleased.

The two boys turned toward each other then back to Ally and Jane and shook their heads firmly. "Not twins," one of them said.

"Cousins," explained the other.

Then, a moment later, they both added, "Biologically."

"Cousins?" Jane repeated with doubt. "But you look so much alike."

"Our fathers are identical twins," the boys said at the same time.

"Therefore *we* are identical," the first boy said. "That's logic."

"But that's not logical at all," Jane started to argue.

"Of course it is," the second boy insisted. "Logically."

"Did you say something about a party?" Ally prompted, changing the topic before Jane had a chance to protest again.

"Not just any party," the boys said, sounding annoyed by the question. "The mayors' unbirthday party. Plainly."

"You mean a *birthday* party," Jane said.

"Oh, no," one of the boys replied.

"We mean an *un*birthday party," the other continued.

"What is that?" Jane asked.

The two boys looked delighted by her question. They stood up straight, cleared their throats, and announced with an official tone, "The History of the Unbirthday Party!" Then, a moment later, they burst into a bouncy song, complete with a little dance that bobbed them up and down.

> *"The birthday is a sad event, for it comes but once*
> *a year.*
> *The unbirthday is much more fun and full of*
> *much more cheer.*
> *In Tweedleton, we see no sense to wait to*
> *celebrate.*
> *So every day at half past twelve we stop and eat*
> *some cake."*

The boys opened their mouths to sing yet another verse and Ally knew she had to put a stop to this. She had no idea how long the song might continue and she really needed to move the conversation along. She had to get information about the watch so she could figure out how to stop the White Rabbit from ruining the rest of Spirit Weekend.

"Very lovely!" she interrupted them, clapping loudly. "Now, did I hear you say it was the unbirthday party for the *mayor*?"

The mayor of Tweedleton sounded like the perfect person to talk to about the watch. Certainly he or she would know a lot about white rabbits and pocket watches.

"Mayors," the boys corrected, once again sounding annoyed by Ally's ignorance.

"You have more than one mayor?" Jane asked, confused.

"We have two," one of the boys said.

"Our fathers," the other boy explained.

Then they shared a look and at the same time added, "Constitutionally."

"Your fathers are the mayors?" Ally confirmed.

"Positively," the boys replied.

Ally turned to Jane and bent her head close to whisper, "Perhaps we should ask *them* about the pocket watch. If their fathers are the mayors, maybe they'll know the connection between the White Rabbit and the watch."

Jane looked like she was about to respond, but then both girls noticed the boys leaning in close to try to overhear their conversation.

"It's not polite to eavesdrop on people's conversations," Ally told them in a stern voice.

"It's not polite to whisper," one of the boys responded without missing a beat. "Certainly."

"I suppose that's true," Ally reasoned.

"It's not true. It's manners," the boys said in unison.

Ally sighed and pulled the broken watch from the pocket of her dress. "Okay, fine. We were hoping you could tell us—"

But she never managed to finish the sentence. Because as soon as the boys saw the pocket watch, their eyes grew very, very wide and they let out a concurrent shriek as they darted away from Ally and Jane, heading straight into the forest, with perfectly synchronized steps.

Not So Fast

*If those guys thought they
were getting away easy, they
had another thing coming.*

Ally immediately leapt off the bench and sprinted into the forest after the boys.

"What are you doing?" Jane called after her.

"Following them!" Ally called back.

"Can't we talk to someone else? Those two are kind of strange!"

"They reacted to the broken pocket watch! They clearly know something!"

Ally came upon a clearing with three paths jutting out in three different directions. She stopped to consider her options. Which way had they gone? Had they split up?

She immediately ruled out that possibility. The two were practically joined at the hip. In fact, Ally wondered if maybe they *were* physically joined at the hip. Were conjoined cousins a thing?

She was starting to think that *anything* could be a thing in Tweedleton.

Jane caught up with her, slightly out of breath. "What now?"

"They can't have gone far," Ally reasoned.

"We haven't." The unmistakable sound of the boys' voices seemed to echo all around them, as if the cousins were in a hundred places at once.

Ally painted on a sweet smile. "Can you two please come out? We need to talk to you about the watch."

"We must hide," one of the boys said with a quiver in his voice.

"Why?" Ally asked.

"Because the veil has been broken," was the response.

"What veil?" Ally asked, wandering around the clearing and peering into bushes in search of the boys.

"The veil between Auradon and Wonderland," the boys said together.

Ally paused. She stared down at the pocket watch still in her hand and ran her fingertip over the cracked glass.

The veil has been broken?

"What does that mean?" Ally called into the trees.

"The White Rabbit!" the boys responded, as though the answer were obvious.

Ally's eyebrows sprang up. "What about the White Rabbit?"

"If the veil is broken then he's escaped."

Escaped.

So she was right! There *was* a connection between the White Rabbit being in Auradon and the breaking of this watch.

Ally knew she needed more of an explanation and she was certain these boys could give her one. She just had to figure out a way to lure them out of hiding. Ally tapped her forehead to think, but it was Jane who came up with the answer, as though she were reading Ally's mind.

"Will you sing us a song about the watch?" Jane asked, and she nodded knowingly at Ally.

"A song?" the boys chirped excitedly.

Ally really didn't want to sit through another one of their songs, but she had a feeling Jane's tactic to draw them out was a clever one. "Yes, please," Ally said. "A song would be lovely."

Before she could blink, the boys had reemerged and were standing in front of Jane and Ally. They walked toward them until the girls backed up against a fallen log and had no choice but to sit.

The boys straightened their spines. The first one announced, "The Story of the Magic Pocket Watch." Then the other added, "Or, How the White Rabbit Got Trapped in Wonderland."

With the same playful rhythm and bouncy dance moves, the boys started to sing.

"Once there was a white rabbit, who was always, always late.
He ran from place to place, babbling about a date.
He took no care in what he did or the trouble that he caused.
So the watchmaker sent him home, and everyone applaused."

"I think the word is *applauded*," Jane interrupted.

The two boys shot her aggravated looks at the disruption and Jane quickly tucked her hands in her lap and fell quiet.

They cleared their throats and continued.

*"For the rabbit was the worrying sort, whose
    nerves did bring a stir
To every town and hovel where he shed his tufts
    of fur.
But once the watch was wound, the rabbit was
    safe and locked.
He was forever kept in Wonderland, unless the
    clock be stopped."*

Ally knew she should have applauded—or *applaused*, as it were—at the end of their performance, but she couldn't bring herself to move. She was in too much shock.

A watchmaker had locked the White Rabbit in Wonderland using this pocket watch, and when the watch had stopped, the White Rabbit was let loose. Now he was wreaking havoc in Auradon, eating cakes and stealing watches and ruining signs.

"You were right," Jane said to Ally with wide eyes, "about everything."

Ally wanted to feel pride at hearing Jane say this, but she was too busy trying to put all the pieces together. "He's just been scared," Ally concluded. "The song said he was the 'worrying sort.'"

Jane nodded. "This whole time he's probably been panicked and lost, trying to find his way back home. That's why he's caused all that trouble."

"Trouble is right," one of the boys said, before the other added, "And more trouble he'll bring the longer he's out and about."

"Oh, dear," Ally said, staring down at her lap. "I can't imagine what he'll do next. What if he leaves the school? What if he starts causing trouble all over Auradon?"

The two boys let out another simultaneous shriek of fear before removing their caps and covering their faces with them.

Ally was feeling guiltier than ever about breaking the pocket watch. What else would the White Rabbit do? These boys were clearly very scared of the possibilities. She knew she had to find a way to fix this mess.

"But how do we send him ba—" Ally started to ask, but flinched when the boys suddenly darted into the trees again. There one second and gone the next.

Ally was beginning to understand why her mother didn't like to come to Tweedleton. This town was already making her head spin.

"Oh, dear," Ally said again. "Oh dear, oh dear, oh dear."

"Don't panic," Jane said soothingly. "We'll figure out what to do. We just need to send the White Rabbit back to Wonderland before he does more damage."

"But how?" Ally asked, feeling helpless.

Jane bit her lip, thinking. "In the song, the boys said the watchmaker sent him home and 'once the watch was wound, the rabbit was safe and locked.'"

"'He was forever kept in Wonderland, unless the clock be stopped,'" Ally continued the rhyme. She turned the watch over and once again traced the letters of the engraving on the back. "The watchmaker in the song must refer to this Mr. Weiden fellow."

"Yes, but Mr. Weiden didn't come up in the search," Jane reminded her.

Ally tapped her forehead. "Maybe we don't need

that watchmaker. Maybe we just need *a* watchmaker."

"Any watchmaker?" Jane asked.

Ally grew excited as the realization hit her. "Yes! Exactly! We need to *fix* the pocket watch. If breaking it let the White Rabbit out . . ."

Jane caught on immediately and finished Ally's thought as smoothly as if they were identical cousins. "Then fixing it would send him back home."

Ally smiled. "Naturally."

CLOCK IN

Clotted cream balls! We needed to get to that watchmaker, and quickly!

The two girls found their way back into the main square of the town, which was now bustling with people and activity. Apparently, the mayors' unbirthday party was over. They scanned the names of the shops again, this time searching for one that said *watchmaker*.

"I don't see any watch shops," Jane said with disappointment.

"Let's ask someone," Ally suggested. "There has to be a watchmaker in town." She surveyed her surroundings before her gaze finally settled on a sign that read HATTER'S SOCK SHOP.

Ally led the way and Jane followed as they entered

the shop to find an older gentleman sitting behind the counter. He had wispy snow-white hair sprouting in every direction from his head.

"Customers!" the man said, standing up quickly. But the sudden movement caused his wild hair to fall into his eyes. He grunted with frustration, wet his fingertips, and attempted to slick back the unruly locks. The hair flopped right back into his face.

Ally glanced around the shop. It was filled with shelves upon shelves of every kind of sock imaginable: argyle, striped, polka-dotted, woolen, cotton. Even tiny socks for dogs and cats.

How odd that someone named Hatter would sell socks.

"What can I do for you, lovely ladies?" the man said, and Ally's attention was brought back to the counter.

She smiled her most polite smile and said, "We're looking for a watchmaker. Is there one in town?"

The man shook his head, his hair drooping into his eyes again. "Afraid not. Old Mr. Thumpkins retired a few years back. He was the only watchmaker in town, but his store got turned into a croquet shop."

Ally felt her chest squeeze. "Oh, no. That's not

good. Not good at all. You see, we have this pocket watch and it needs to be fixed."

The man's entire face lit up as he once again tried and failed to tame his disobedient hair. "I fix watches!"

"You do?" Ally asked, pleased with her instinct to come into this particular shop.

"Absolutely!" the man said. "Is it a mad watch?"

Jane and Ally exchanged befuddled looks.

"A *mad* watch?" Ally repeated.

"Yes," Mr. Hatter confirmed. "Has it gone mad? Insane? Kooky? Wacky? Deranged?"

"Uh, no," Ally replied cautiously. "I mean, I don't think it's mad. I think it's just broken. Its heart stopped."

"Tsk, tsk, tsk," the man said, with sorrow in his eyes. "How very sad."

"Isn't it, though?" Ally asked. It was a relief to finally feel understood by someone.

"Very sad, indeed," Mr. Hatter said as his eyes started to water. He pulled a handkerchief from his pocket and blew his nose so loudly that both girls had to cover their ears to block the horrendous sound. When he was finished, his hair was even more disheveled than before. He wet his fingertips again and tried to smooth it down, but the strands just sprung right back into place. "Well, I'm sorry I can't help you, miss," he offered. "I only fix *mad* watches."

Ally sighed, feeling her hopes vanish again. "Is there anyone in town who fixes *broken* watches?"

"Broken watches?" The man jumped to attention. "Well, of course. Old man Thumpkins fixes broken watches. He's the watchmaker."

Ally bit her lip, trying not to get discouraged. "Yes, but I thought you just said he's retired."

"Oh, he is," Mr. Hatter replied. "Closed up his place a few years ago. Now it's a croquet shop."

"Yes, you said already," Ally reminded him, growing frustrated. They were wasting precious time going round and round in circles.

"He'll fix your watch right up!" Mr. Hatter said, seemingly not hearing her.

"But how can he do that if he's retired?" Jane asked.

"He's retired," the man said, "not *dead*. He still fixes watches out of his home."

And just like that, Ally's hopes took flight again. "Well, where does he live?"

"Right outside of town," the man replied. "Just follow the path." His hair fell back into his face and he groaned and pressed down hard on his head, like he was trying to squash the hair into submission. But as soon as he lifted his hands, his hair was a mess again.

"Thank you!" Ally exclaimed.

"Yes, thank you!" Jane echoed.

The girls started for the door, but suddenly, Ally had a thought and turned back to the man behind the counter. "You know," she said delicately, "a hat would probably really help your, um, hair situation."

Mr. Hatter stopped futzing with his hair for a moment, looking pensive. "A hat?" he repeated, curious. "You don't say! What a splendid idea!" Then he cupped his hands and called toward the back of the shop, "Mrs. Hatter! From now on, we shall be selling only hats!"

Jane and Ally glanced at each other before breaking into uncontrollable giggles and running from the shop.

CUCKOO TIME

Old Mr. Thumpkins's house was
shaped like a giant alarm clock,
which was perfectly fitting for
the wacky watchmaker.

When the girls knocked on the door, Ally expected to
see a tubby old man with a monocle appear. But the
reality of the situation was much different.

Mr. Thumpkins was tall and lean and muscular. If
he was old, it only showed in the slight wrinkles around
his eyes, the gray tint of his hair, and the gentle sag of
the skin on his neck. The rest of his body was trim, fit,
and toned.

And within a moment of his answering the door,
Ally and Jane understood why.

"Today's the day!" he said, darting out the door and doing a quick leg stretch. He pressed the button on a stopwatch in his hand and then he was off. He ran to the end of the short walkway that led from the main road up to his house, opened the mailbox, pulled out a stack of envelopes, closed the mailbox, and sprinted back. The whole thing happened so fast, Ally struggled to comprehend what was going on. When he returned, he punched the stopwatch again and looked eagerly at the time. He threw up his hands and celebrated. "Wahoo! Beat it!"

"Beat what?" Ally asked, intrigued.

He turned the stopwatch around to show the girls. The number 00:00:05.88 was on the screen. "Yesterday, I got the mail in five point nine two seconds. Do you know what that means?"

Jane leaned forward and studied the watch. "Today you were faster?" she guessed.

He threw his hands up in the air again. "Today I was faster! Wahoo!" He beckoned the girls inside. "Come, come in. I'll make us some tea."

Mr. Thumpkins punched the stopwatch again and ushered the girls into the house. He seemed to be herding them like sheep. When he finally shut the door behind them, he stopped the watch. His face fell into a frown. "Hmmm. One point three five seconds slower than the last guests I had. You girls need to learn to pick up the pace!"

Jane and Ally exchanged another curious glance. They'd been doing that a lot since they came to Tweedleton. The town and the people in it were certainly peculiar.

Ally peered around inside the house. Every single surface was covered with clocks. The walls, the shelves, the bookcases. There were even clocks glued to the ceiling. The noise was a bit distracting.

The watchmaker led them through the living room into the kitchen.

"So you like to time things?" Ally asked, taking it all in.

"Wait!" Mr. Thumpkins said, resetting his stopwatch. He pressed start and then he was off again, filling a teapot with water, lighting the stove, dropping loose tea leaves into cups, and arranging spoons on a tray. When he was done, he stopped the watch and looked at it. "A world record!"

"A world record?" Ally repeated. "That's impressive."

The man waved her compliment away. "Oh, it's nothing. Just me filling a teapot faster than any person in recorded history."

"They have a recorded history of that?" Jane sounded skeptical.

"Of course they do!" Mr. Thumpkins replied.

"Yes, *of course* they do," Ally repeated, shooting Jane a look. She turned back to the watchmaker. "You'll have to excuse her. She's much too logical for her own good."

The man laughed like this was the funniest thing he'd ever heard. "Oh, we don't have much use for logic around here."

Ally grinned. "Then this is my kind of place!"

Jane just rolled her eyes.

"Anyway," Ally went on, "we were hoping you could help us."

The watchmaker leaned forward, suddenly looking extremely interested. "Help you? I love helping people. What can I do for you? Does it require timing something?"

"It could." Ally pulled out the broken pocket watch. She half expected Mr. Thumpkins to react the same way the identical cousins had reacted—shrieking and running off to hide somewhere—but instead he just smiled.

"We were hoping you could fix this," Ally went on. "You see, I broke it—well, actually my cat broke it, but he won't admit to that."

"Not surprising," the man said with a nod. "Cats are dreadful at accepting blame."

"Exactly," Ally continued. "So I tried to find Mr. Weiden to have *him* fix it but—"

"Mr. who?" the man interrupted.

"Weiden. The watch's original maker."

The man cocked his head to the side, like he was thinking hard about something. "Hmmm. That name doesn't ring a bell. I could have sworn I knew all the watchmakers in Auradon."

Ally shrugged. "No matter. I couldn't find him anyway. So we were hoping *you* could fix it."

"Of course I can fix it!"

"You can?"

The man brushed invisible crumbs from his shirt. "Well, I am the watchmaker. Fixing watches is what I . . ." His voice trailed off as he seemed to get lost in thought again. "Well, I guess technically *making* watches is what I do. But I do fix them, as well. Maybe I should change my title to 'watchfixer.' But that just doesn't have the same ring to it, does it?"

Just then, the water in the kettle started to boil, filling the small kitchen with a sharp whistle.

"Ring!" the watchmaker called out, punching his stopwatch again. "And go!" He grabbed the kettle and speedily filled the teacups. When he was finished he stopped the watch, frowning. "Hmmm. Better luck next time." He offered cups to the girls and blew on his own before taking a sip. "Mmmm. Delicious tea."

"So," Ally said, trying to bring his attention back to the problem at hand. "The broken pocket watch."

"Ah, yes!" the man cried out, as though he'd completely forgotten about it already. "I can fix it in record time!"

Ally beamed at Jane. "That would be great!"

"Let me just finish my tea," the watchmaker said, starting his stopwatch and then downing the tea in one giant gulp. But it must have been too hot, because he choked and clawed at his throat, dropping his stopwatch in the process.

"Are you all right?" Ally asked, concerned.

The man's eyes went wide and red and he looked like he was trying to say something. But all that came out was raspy garbles. "Chullucharararachura!"

"What?" Ally asked. "What is it?" She turned to Jane. "What's he saying?"

Jane shook her head. "I don't know but it looks like he's pointing at something."

The girls peered at the man, who was indeed pointing desperately at something.

"Water?" Ally guessed. "Do you need some cold water?"

He shook his head and pointed at the floor, still trying and failing to speak. "Gluhhhmuhhhrahhhblahh!" he cried.

"What's he pointing at?" Jane asked.

Ally followed the direction of his finger until her eyes fell on the stopwatch on the floor. She picked it up. "Is this what you want?"

Mr. Thumpkins nodded emphatically, still clutching his throat. "Stahhhihhh!"

Ally squinted. "What?"

He let out a horrific ragged cough and tried again. "Staaaahhh pihhh!"

Ally looked to Jane. "Do you know what he's saying?"

Jane shook her head. "I don't speak Crazy Watchmaker."

"Stahhhp ihhht," he said again, this time with somewhat more clarity.

Ally glanced down at the stopwatch in her hand. The timer was still going from when he'd tried to time himself drinking the tea. "Oh!" she said. "You want me to stop the timer?"

He nodded and smiled.

Ally punched down on the button and the timer came to a halt. She turned it around to show him. "Twenty seven point eight two seconds."

He pumped the air with his fist and cleared his throat, finally finding his voice again. "Yes! That's two seconds faster than last time!"

Ally was beyond confused. But before she could question him, he grabbed the broken pocket watch from the counter and beckoned for the girls to follow him. "To the workshop!"

With a Quickness

I needed Mr. Thumpkins to hurry. I had to get back to Auradon before the White Rabbit did any more damage!

Mr. Thumpkins was right. He *did* fix the watch in record time. Not that Ally had anything to measure it against. She had never seen a watchmaker fix a watch before, but he certainly *seemed* to be moving fast. Before Ally could even blink, he had the glass face off and was tinkering around inside with a bunch of tiny tools Ally had never seen before. Then he zoomed to the other side of his workshop and turned on a loud machine that quickly cut a new piece of glass from a larger sheet.

Once the glass was cut, he secured it to the front

of the watch with a click and handed the fixed device over to Ally. "There you are! Good as new!"

Ally immediately pressed the watch to her ear and listened. A moment later, she heard it: *tick, tick, tick*. She breathed a sigh of relief. "You did it! You brought it back to life!"

The watchmaker beamed. "Nice strong heartbeat it's got there, too. A mighty fine watch. I'd love to know who made it."

Ally chuckled. "I told you. Mr. Weiden!"

The watchmaker looked confused for a moment. "Huh. Okay. Well, if you figure out who made the watch, you let me know, okay?"

Ally just shook her head. She was starting to understand how the other students at Auradon felt about *her*. This man definitely lived on a planet of his own. In fact, all the people in this town did.

"Oh! I almost forgot," Mr. Thumpkins said, taking the pocket watch back from Ally. He glanced up at one of the hundreds of clocks on his wall and began to wind her pocket watch forward to the correct time. Then he handed it back. "There you go. All synced up."

Ally peered at the hands of her mum's beautiful

golden pocket watch. The hour hand was pointed at the five and the minute hand was pointed at . . .

"Crumbs!" Ally swore, looking up at Jane with panic in her eyes. "It's almost five thirty! The concert starts in an hour and a half! We have to go!"

The girls thanked Mr. Thumpkins profusely before running out the door and through the town, hopping back on their bike, and starting the long journey back to Auradon Prep.

Maybe it was because they were in a hurry. Or maybe it was because they'd had more than two hours of practice on the way to Tweedleton, but the ride back to Auradon Prep was much easier. Ally took the front seat and steered. She didn't utter a single complaint about Jane's lack of effort in the back. And Jane pedaled fast and furiously, without once mentioning Ally's steering abilities.

Ally noticed how much more enjoyable a ride it was when the two of them weren't bickering. In fact, she even went so far as to think the whole field trip had been *fun*. Peculiar, but fun. And she was glad Jane had accidentally turned that cucumber into a tandem bike instead of a regular bike. She was glad that Jane had come along. The adventure would have been quite lonely without her friend.

When they got back to the school, Ally steered them toward the tea shop, passing right by the tourney field, but she brought the bike to a screeching stop when she saw the catastrophe that lay in front of them.

Frosted tea cakes!

Ally immediately jumped off the bike and ran to the edge of the tourney field to survey the damage. As she scanned the ground, she saw the entire field was covered in holes. It was as if someone had gone out there with a shovel and dug a thousand little craters in the grass. Each hole was no wider than Ally's foot, but the sum of all the holes was pretty disastrous.

Ally spotted Mal standing in the center of the field, surveying the damage with her hands on her hips. Ally carefully made her way over, walking on her tiptoes to avoid twisting an ankle in one of the shallow holes.

"What happened?" Ally asked breathlessly.

"I don't know!" Mal screamed, sounding extremely agitated and stressed. "Everything was set and ready. The band was about to arrive. I went inside to have dinner and I came back out and I found this!" She spread her arms wide. "I don't understand who would even do this! And how am I supposed to fix it? I can't fill all of these holes in time. There's no way we can have the concert here!"

"It's fine," Ally said, trying to comfort her. "We can still sit here. We'll just be a little lopsided." She had tried for a joke, but Mal didn't laugh. In fact, she barely even glanced at Ally.

"Yeah," Mal replied bitterly. "We can sit on this, but Talking Dragons can't play on *that*."

Mal pointed toward the opposite end of the tourney field and Ally followed the direction of her finger with dread in her stomach. The stage Mal had spent days setting up for that night's show was now slanted at an awkward angle. It appeared so many holes had been dug around it that the ground beneath the stage had given way. The stage was literally sinking into the field.

The first thought to flicker through Ally's mind was: *We were too late. The White Rabbit must have done this before Mr. Thumpkins fixed the watch. If we had only pedaled faster or argued less or left sooner . . .*

Mal let out a frustrated sigh. "Now the band is packing up. They're going to leave soon and my big surprise for Ben is ruined. I can't believe this."

Ally bit her lip, not knowing what to do. She'd never seen Mal so upset before. Ally glanced over at the road, where a bunch of guys were loading instruments and equipment into a van. Written on the side of the van were the words TALKING DRAGONS.

"You know," Ally said, trying to keep her voice light, "Talking Dragons is an anagram for 'a dangling stork.'"

She was hoping the word game would cheer Mal up, the way it always cheered Ally up when she was upset or feeling down. But it didn't seem to work. Mal just let out a huff and started to walk away.

And that's when Ally knew that she had really, truly failed. She'd wanted so badly to avoid this. She'd wanted to fix everything. But she was too slow. Too late. She pulled the pocket watch from her pocket and stared at it. It was six thirty.

Wow, Ally mused. She and Jane had really gotten back in record time. It had taken them two hours to get to Tweedleton but only an hour to get back.

She knew it was only an hour, because when Mr. Thumpkins wound the clock forward to sync the time, he'd set it for five thirty.

Five thirty?

Ally's eyebrows shot up and she chased after Mal, who was already halfway across the cratered field. "Mal!" she said urgently.

Mal stopped and turned to glare at Ally. "What?" she snapped.

"When did you say you went inside?"

"It was dinnertime," Mal said. "Dinner is always at six."

"And the field looked normal when you left it?"

"Yeah," Mal said, growing impatient. "Perfectly normal. Why?"

But Ally didn't answer her. Her mind was too busy reeling.

It didn't work.

We fixed the watch but the White Rabbit is still out there. That's probably why he dug all of these holes. He's still trying to get home to Wonderland.

"Ally?" Mal said, interrupting Ally's thoughts. She sounded slightly suspicious. "Do you know anything about this?"

But once again, Ally didn't answer. She took off at a run, carefully weaving around the holes in the grass until she reached Jane, who was waiting with the bike.

"It didn't work," she told Jane breathlessly.

"What do you mean it didn't work?"

Ally gestured to the field. "The White Rabbit did this"—she fought to catch her breath—"*after* Mr. Thumpkins fixed the watch. We didn't send him home. He's still here."

Jane rubbed her eyes, clearly trying to make sense of this. "I don't get it. If fixing the watch didn't send him home, what will?"

Ally shook her head. "I don't know. I thought . . ." Her eyes pricked with tears. She had done it again. She had made the wrong assumption. She had jumped to the wrong conclusion. "I messed up," she blubbered. "I'm always *always* messing up. I can't get anything right."

She expected Jane to reprimand her again. To tell her she was a lousy detective and should just spend her days baking cakes and pouring tea. But Jane didn't say any of that. Instead, she put a gentle hand on Ally's shoulder and said, "No, that's not true. You can do this. I believe in you. If anyone can figure this out, it's you. You're the best detective I know."

Ally sniffled. "I'm the only detective you know."

Jane giggled. "That's true. But even if I knew a hundred detectives, you'd still probably be the best."

"No. No, I wouldn't. I can't even solve a single mystery! I just keep misinterpreting the clues."

"But that's what makes you interesting!" Jane said. "Because you see things differently. You look at the world differently. It's like your superpower."

"But what good does that do me now?" Ally asked. "The concert is ruined. The White Rabbit is still out there, and I don't know how to send him back."

"Well," Jane said, "let's just slow down and think about this logically. You broke the watch and that let the White Rabbit out. What else could possibly send him home?"

Ally huffed and threw up her hands. "I don't know! I thought that fixing the watch would do it. But maybe it was the wrong watchmaker. Maybe the original watchmaker from the song has to fix it. The one who locked the White Rabbit in Wonderland in the first place. That Mr. Deiwen person."

"Mr. Weiden," Jane corrected.

Ally shook her head and stared at Jane as though she were out of focus. "What are you talking about?"

"The name on the back of the watch," Jane clarified. "It's Mr. Weiden. Not Mr. Deiwen. You mixed up the letters."

Ally pulled the watch from her pocket again. "No, I didn't. Look, it says—" But she stopped when she realized that Jane was right. There it was, engraved right into the back.

MR WEIDEN

Ally had rearranged the letters, just like she always did. Except this time, she'd done it unconsciously.

"See," Jane said, giving Ally's shoulders a squeeze. "I told you. You see the world differently. You even see *words* differently."

"Yes, but—" Ally's sentence was cut off by a loud gasp. It came from her own lips. She covered her mouth with her hands as she stared down at the watch, still clutched in her hands.

"Jane!" Ally cried out, causing Jane to look slightly scared for a moment.

"What?"

Ally grabbed Jane's arm and shook it. "JANE!"

"WHAT?" Jane repeated.

"You're a genius!"

Jane looked puzzled. "I am?"

"See the words differently," Ally echoed Jane's previous comment. "Of course! How could I not realize it before? I spend most of my day rearranging letters."

Jane still didn't appear to be catching on. "What are you talking about?"

Ally held up the watch. " 'Mr. Weiden' isn't the name of the watchmaker. It's not a name at all." Then Ally grinned the biggest grin she'd ever grinned and said, "It's an anagram!"

KEEPS ON TICKIN'

*If it was truly an anagram, then
I knew I could solve it. I just had
to think, think, <u>think</u>. . . .*

For the next few minutes, Ally tapped her forehead and tried to come up with every possible combination of words she could think of using the letters found in "Mr. Weiden."

"Wed miner."

Tap. Tap. Tap.

"Weird men."

Tap. Tap. Tap.

"Windmere."

"Drew mine."

"Remind we."

"Re*wind* me."

Ally stopped, the last combination echoing loudly in her mind, like a series of clanging bells.

"Rewind me," she repeated. "Drink me. Eat me. Rewind me!" Ally's mouth fell open.

But once the watch was wound, the rabbit was safe and locked.

"Of course! The cousins' song. 'Once the watch was wound, the rabbit was safe and locked.' Watches are wound forward *and* back. The answer has been written here all along. The engraving is telling us to rewind the pocket watch!"

Ally expected Jane to look as ecstatic as Ally felt. But she saw only confusion in Jane's eyes.

"Wait. Why?" Jane asked.

But Ally was already turning the little knob on the side of the watch, back and back and back. "Don't you see?" Ally said. "The watch broke at one thirty p.m. yesterday. We have to wind it back to exactly that time to send the rabbit home."

Jane frowned. She wasn't following. "That doesn't make any sense."

"Of course it does. It makes *Wonderland* sense. It's Ally logic!"

Ally turned and turned until the small hand had been rewound twenty-nine hours, the amount of time that had passed since Ally had broken the watch the day before.

And then . . .

Very peculiar things started to happen.

The pocket watch began to hum. Softly at first, but getting louder and louder with every *tick, tick, tick* of the second hand. Then the entire watch lit up with a bright orange glow. Ally was so startled she nearly dropped it and broke it all over again. But she kept it firmly clutched between her fingers as both girls watched the glowing object in wonderment.

"Holy dragons!" a voice cried out, and Ally's eyes darted back toward the tourney field where Mal still stood. Except she didn't look angry anymore. Now her mouth was open in astonishment as she gazed across the field.

Something was happening to the grass.

The holes were filling right before their very eyes.

Ally's heart started to thud in her chest as the realization hit her. "The watch. It's reversing everything the White Rabbit did!"

The girls looked on in amazement as the holes

finished filling with dirt and the giant stage, which had been sitting lopsided just a moment before, slowly started to right itself, like a sleeping giant rising from a nap.

Mal clapped giddily, but the sudden sound of a door slamming shut snapped her out of her celebration. She turned to see the musicians getting into the Talking Dragons van, about to pull away. "Oh, no! I have to tell the band the concert is back on!" She took off toward the road.

Ally had a sudden thought of her own and started running. She dashed straight to the royal hall and burst through the front doors. Jane was right behind her, clearly understanding what she was doing.

And there it was. Sitting in the center of the table was Ally's cake. Beautiful. Towering. Frosted white. And completely untouched.

"What about my watch?" Jane asked eagerly, her eyes alight.

The two girls took off again, running toward the dorms. When they burst into Jane's room, Jane immediately looked to the top of her dresser and let out a shriek. "My mom's watch! It's back!" She grabbed it and fastened it to her wrist, tilting her arm this way and that to admire it. She bent down to kiss it. "Thank you! Thank you! Thank you!"

Then she turned to Ally. "Thank *you*."

Ally shrugged. "Oh, it was nothing."

"It wasn't nothing," Jane argued. "You did it. You solved the mystery of the White Rabbit!"

"The *mad* mystery is more like it," Ally said with a sigh. Then the two girls broke into fits of triumphant giggles.

WATCH OUT

I did it! Nothing can stop me!
I proved I'm really a detective.
And now everybody knows it!

The drummer of Talking Dragons beat his drumsticks together three times and launched into the final song of the night. It was a loud, rocking number and everyone at Auradon Prep was on their feet, jumping up and down, and singing along.

Ally stood in the back of the crowd, watching all her classmates enjoy the show. The look on Ben's face as Talking Dragons had taken the stage earlier *was* pretty priceless. It made Ally feel warm and fuzzy all over.

She'd done it. She'd saved the day. Well, she'd had help from a friend. A very good friend.

Ally slipped her hand into her pocket and touched the pocket watch. Her family heirloom.

Once the watch was wound, the rabbit was safe and locked.

He was forever kept in Wonderland, unless the clock be stopped.

And at that moment, as the band hit the first chorus and the crowd went wild, Ally made a promise. She would take care of this watch. She would never let anything happen to it again.

She would protect it, just as her mother had for all those years. Because she now understood just how important it was to keep that watch's heart beating strong.

"They're pretty wicked, aren't they?" Mal said, coming up next to Ally and bumping her hip against Ally's to the beat of the music.

Ally hadn't expected to see Mal. She'd thought Mal would be up in the front with Ben. "What are you doing back here?" Ally asked.

"Thanking you," Mal said. She put an arm around Ally, surprising her. "Jane told me what you did. She told everyone. You saved this concert. You saved this school. You're pretty much my hero right now."

"Hero?" Ally choked out, the word barely making it past her lips.

"Yes," said another voice, and Ally turned to see Fairy Godmother approach with Jane trailing right behind her. "Hero." Fairy Godmother smiled her warm, motherly smile. "While I don't approve of the two of you sneaking off like that, I have to say I'm proud of you." She turned back and opened her arms to Jane. "Both of you."

Jane stepped into her mother's embrace and snuggled up close to her. Then the most peculiar thing happened. Fairy Godmother started to dance! She unbuttoned her blazer and raised her hands in the air, letting out a "Whoop, whoop!"

Mal, Ally, and Jane all broke out laughing, but it didn't deter the headmistress. The music had overtaken her and she was now dancing her heart out.

Jane sidled up next to Ally. "Well," she said with a sigh. "That was exciting, huh? I guess we can finally get some rest now that the case is solved."

"Yeah," Ally agreed with a mournful sigh. Although she was happy to have solved the case and saved the day, she was also a little sad that it was all over. This was the end. What would she do now?

But as soon as the question popped into her head, she realized the answer was obvious. What do all detectives do when they finish up a case? They start another one!

And that's exactly what Ally intended to do.

As she glanced around the packed tourney field, watching her friends and classmates rock out to the music of Talking Dragons, there was no doubt in Ally's mind that she'd eventually find another case.

As long as there was magic, there would always be mysteries to solve in Auradon.

Check out all of the
SCHOOL OF SECRETS
books!